PRAISE

#1 NEW YORK ...

MW01287503

BARBARA FREETHY

"In the tradition of LaVyrle Spencer, gifted author Barbara Freethy creates an irresistible tale of family secrets, riveting adventure and heart- touching romance."

*-- NYT Bestselling Author **Susan Wiggs***
on Summer Secrets

"This book has it all: heart, community, and characters who' will remain with you long after the book has ended. A wonderful story."

*-- NYT Bestselling Author **Debbie Macomber***
on Suddenly One Summer

"Freethy has a gift for creating complex characters."

*-- **Library Journal***

"Barbara Freethy is a master storyteller with a gift for spinning tales about ordinary people in extraordinary situations and drawing readers into their lives."

*-- **Romance Reviews Today***

"Freethy's skillful plotting and gift for creating sympathetic characters will ensure that few dry eyes will be left at the end of the story."

*-- **Publishers Weekly** on The Way Back Home*

"Freethy skillfully keeps the reader on the hook, and her tantalizing and believable tale has it all– romance, adventure, and mystery."

*-- **Booklist** on Summer Secrets*

"Freethy's story-telling ability is top-notch."

*-- **Romantic Times** on Don't Say A Word*

Also By Barbara Freethy

Lightning Strikes Trilogy
Beautiful Storm (#1)
Lightning Lingers (#2)
Summer Rain (#3)

The Callaway Series
On A Night Like This (#1)
So This Is Love (#2)
Falling For A Stranger (#3)
Between Now and Forever (#4)
Nobody But You (Callaway Wedding Novella)
All A Heart Needs (#5)
That Summer Night (#6)
When Shadows Fall (#7)
Somewhere Only We Know (#8)
If I Didn't Know Better (#9)
Tender Is The Night (#10)
Take Me Home (A Callaway Novella)
Closer To You (#11) *Coming Soon!*

The Wish Series
A Secret Wish
Just A Wish Away
When Wishes Collide

Standalone Novels
Almost Home
All She Ever Wanted
Ask Mariah
Daniel's Gift
Don't Say A Word
Golden Lies
Just The Way You Are
Love Will Find A Way
One True Love
Ryan's Return
Some Kind of Wonderful
Summer Secrets
The Sweetest Thing

The Sanders Brothers Series
Silent Run & Silent Fall

The Deception Series
Taken & Played

Also Available

7 Brides for 7 Brothers

LUKE

7 Brides for 7 Brothers

—➤➤❮❮❮—

BARBARA FREETHY

HYDE
STREET
—PRESS—

HYDE STREET PRESS
Published by Hyde Street Press
1325 Howard Avenue, #321
Burlingame, California 94010

Printed in the United States of America

Cover design by Damonza.com

ISBN: 978-1-9437813-6-2

One

"**W**inds are picking up," Luke Brannigan muttered, as he adjusted the camera on his helmet and prepared for his jump off the infamous Kjeragbolten boulder on the mountain Kjerag in Norway, one of the most extreme base jumping locations in the world. He'd been planning this jump for weeks. It would be the centerpiece of his next documentary film on extreme sports, but unfortunately the weather was starting to threaten his ambitious plan.

"I'm sure you're still jumping," Pete Ramsay said knowingly, as he readied the drone that would film Luke's free-falling jump off the mountain. "The word abort is not in your vocabulary."

Pete knew him well. Once he had his eyes set on a goal, he rarely backed down. In fact, he couldn't remember the last time he had bailed out of anything, but he had a churning feeling in his gut. In fact, that feeling had been there for days, and he didn't quite know what it was all about, but he didn't have time to figure it out.

"Now or not today," Pete said, tension in his tone, as their gazes met.

"Let's make it now," he said decisively. "I'll see you at the bottom. Get ready to buy me a beer."

"You've got it. Good luck."

"I don't need luck. I'm prepared." He double-checked his rig and then climbed down onto the infamous boulder that hung between two cliffs some four thousand feet above a deep abyss. He looked up at Pete, held up his hand and counted down on his fingers: three-two-one.

Then he jumped.

He'd free-fallen many times before, but it was impossible to get used to the exhilarating terror-filled adrenaline rush, the speed of flight, the magnificent view, and then the feeling of incredible calm and clarity. Nothing else mattered. He was on a cloud. He was in the heavens and his real life was far, far away.

It was such a spectacular feeling that he wanted to hold on to it, to keep flying forever.

But the wind was stronger today, and he could feel it pushing him back toward the cliffs. He had to fight to stay free of the perilous rocks. With his brain once again engaged in saving his own life, he launched the chute that would stop him from dying.

The parachute yanked him back up into the sky, and then he had only a few seconds more to enjoy the ride. The wind blew him a little off course, but he managed to find solid earth to set down on.

When his feet touched the ground, he waited for the usual mix of joyous relief and intense sadness that often accompanied his adventures: relief that he'd cheated death once again and sadness that the experience was over, that nothing that felt that good could last very long.

But today he felt—different. He didn't know why. He didn't feel nearly as good or even as bad as he normally did. Instead, he just felt…tired.

Shaking his head, he repacked his chute and told himself he just needed a break. He'd been working on this film for the past seven months, traveling all over the world to both capture and perform some of the most incredible death-defying feats in the world.

Normally, he liked waking up in a different city each day, but the transient quality of his life was beginning to get stale. It was ironic that boredom was setting in when it was the very thing he tried to avoid by moving around so frequently.

A fellow jumper landed not too far away from him, interrupting his thoughts. As she pulled off her helmet, her blonde hair fell free, and for just a split second his heart squeezed in anticipation, but it wasn't Lizzie's face that he saw. It wasn't her sky-blue eyes that met his. It wasn't her sexy mouth, her sun-warmed skin with the freckles that dotted her nose in the summer.

This woman was a stranger—just another adrenaline junkie like himself.

She gave him an exhilarated smile. "That was amazing," she said.

"It was," he agreed, watching as a man landed not too far away and quickly ran over to join the woman. The two embraced, and he felt another tug at his heart.

There'd been a time when he'd thought that might be him and Lizzie…that they'd travel the world together. What a crazy thought that had been.

Frowning, he shook his head. *Damn! What the hell was wrong with him?*

He and Lizzie had broken up ten years ago. He'd been twenty then, and he'd just passed his thirtieth birthday last week. Maybe that's why he felt so unsettled. His twenties were gone. It was a new decade.

A better decade than the last one, he told himself firmly, as he walked toward the parking lot. Pete would hike back down the mountain, which would take a few hours. In the meantime, he'd go back to the hotel and run through the film he'd shot until they met up for dinner and that beer Pete owed him.

He was just getting into his car when his phone rang.

The area code for Calabasas, California gave him a jolt. Calabasas was home—or at least the home he'd grown up in…he hadn't actually been to the house there in years. But it wasn't his father's number flashing across the screen.

He answered with a short and automatically wary, "Hello?"

"Luke, it's Aunt Claire."

"Is everything all right?" He knew even before she replied that everything was not okay.

"No," she said heavily.

His gut tightened. "What's happened?"

"It's your father, Luke."

"What about him?"

"I don't know how to say this without it hurting, so I'm just going to give it to you straight." She drew in a breath. "Your father is dead."

His blood roared through his veins so loud he wasn't sure he had heard her right. His dad was only sixty-seven years old, and he was always healthy, always strong, and always bigger than life. He couldn't possibly be dead.

His stomach churned. His head spun, and he had to force himself to take a breath.

"Luke, are you there?" Claire asked, worry in her voice. "I'm sorry to just dump it on you like that. I'm still in shock myself."

"I don't understand. How did it happen? When? Was it an accident?" He had a million questions, but he'd start with those.

"He passed away four days ago. It wasn't an accident; your father had cancer. It was a rare and aggressive cancer. He only got the diagnosis a month ago."

He started shaking his head in confusion. "He got diagnosed a month ago?" he echoed. "Why didn't anyone tell me?"

"No one knew, honey. Your dad said he was taking an extended vacation at his property in the Bahamas. He went there the day after he saw the doctor, and I didn't find out until a week ago when he called me on the phone and swore me to secrecy. He only told me because he wanted me to make sure his wishes were carried out after he passed. I thought about breaking my promise to him and calling you and your brothers, but he was quite adamant that he did not want anyone to watch him die. You know your father. He lived his life on his terms."

He let out a breath, her words jumbling together in his head. "What were his wishes?"

"He wanted to be cremated, and he wanted everything to be done before anyone was told about his death."

"That's crazy," he muttered. "You're saying none of my brothers knew he was sick? No one was there when he died? He was alone?"

"He had hired a couple of nurses on the island and the doctor checked on him each day. He said that after he spoke to me, he was going to call his lawyer, Trent Harper. Trent would take care of the logistical arrangements. But he wanted me to be the one to call you and your brothers and his other friends."

"Who else have you spoken to?"

"You're the first one I've been able to reach."

"So you're saying there's not going to be a funeral of any kind?"

"No. Your dad said he wanted to be remembered as he lived and not as he died. He didn't want some sad ceremony in his honor. He wasn't being selfish, Luke. He was trying to protect all of you."

He wasn't quite as sure of his father's motives as his aunt was. But he was still trying to process the fact that his father was gone. Colin Brannigan was a billionaire, a media industry tycoon, a celebrity, a man with a booming laugh and a love of storytelling, and who lived a fast, loud life. How could a man like that just be gone?

"I'm so sorry, Luke," Claire added. "I know this is a shock. I'm happy to tell you everything I know, but it isn't much. I do have something for you from your dad. Will you be coming home any time soon? It's something I'd like to give you in person."

"I guess," he muttered. "I'm in Norway right now. I'll get a flight tomorrow."

"Call me when you get into town, and we'll meet. Maybe we can get some of your brothers there as well."

"All right."

"I'm sorry again."

He was sorry, too. But he was also pissed. How could his dad die without telling anyone he was sick? It didn't seem that generous to him.

His phone rang again. This time it was Pete.

"I assume you made it," Pete said.

"I did. It was a great ride."

"So we're on for dinner?"

"Actually, no. I need to go home."

Silence followed his words, then Pete said, "Did I hear you right? You need to go home? You—the man who told me you don't even know where home is anymore? What's happened?"

His chest felt too tight to speak the words. "I'll talk to you about it later."

"Are you all right, Luke?"

"I honestly have no idea."

—▸▸◂◂—

Luke arrived in Los Angeles a little after five on Tuesday, the first of September. It was a beautiful Southern California day, not a cloud in the sky, temperature in the eighties, and a shitload of traffic on the 405 freeway. He tapped his fingers impatiently on his thighs as the taxi slowly made its way toward the Santa Monica exit.

He'd been traveling for almost twenty-four hours, and while he needed a shower, a shave, and at least a few hours' sleep, all that would have to wait. He had to meet his aunt first. He needed to learn more about his father's death and find a way to come to terms with it all.

The shocking news still didn't seem true. He was used to being away from his father and the rest of his family for months at a time. He'd spent most of the past ten years traveling, keeping only a small studio apartment in Los Angeles as a home base. For the amount of time he used the place, it probably didn't make sense to pay rent and utilities, but he'd been too busy to consider putting his things in storage. And in between trips, he did need to be in LA to work with editors, producers, and film promoters.

He hadn't seen his father in probably two years, and aside from a few texts and emails every now and then, there had been little communication between them. He and his dad had always lived very separate lives. In fact, there had been many times in his life when he wasn't sure his father even knew of his existence. As the fifth of seven brothers, he'd definitely been lost in the middle of the pack.

His oldest brother James had had the advantage of being born first, not that his solo existence had lasted more than two years. James had been quickly upstaged by the twins Gabe and Hunter, and then Max. Luke had followed, with his two younger brothers, Knox and Finn rounding out the family.

His dad used to say his mom had been determined to have a girl, so they just kept on trying. Unfortunately, she'd never gotten a sweet daughter, just seven wild boys.

Kathleen Brannigan had been a good mom, he thought, feeling an older ache in his chest. There weren't many things he remembered about his mother. She'd died when he was seven years old in a car accident, but in his head he could still see her putting a wriggling worm on a hook as she taught him and Knox how to fish. She definitely hadn't been afraid to get her hands dirty.

A sigh moved his chest as sadness ran through him, a pain made worse now by the loss of his father. Even though he and his dad hadn't always seen eye-to-eye, he'd never thought it would end like this—no words, no warning, no nothing.

His phone vibrated with a text, and he was happy to have a distraction from his thoughts. It was Knox, asking him where he was.

Getting off the freeway, he texted. *Ten minutes.*

After leaving the congested freeway, the taxi made its way up the Pacific Coast Highway to the popular beach city of Santa Monica.

As the cab pulled up in front of the bar where Knox worked, Luke couldn't help but think of the irony of its name—The Wake. Having grown up in an Irish family, he was not unfamiliar with the tradition. Even though his father hadn't wanted a service of any kind, he probably wouldn't mind if they did some reminiscing at a bar.

He paid the cab, then grabbed his duffel bag and backpack out of the trunk and made his way into the building. At a little before six, the bar had a good crowd going, the scarred, weathered tables filled with a mix of surfers, bikers, tourists, and beachgoers, looking for a cool-down after a hot day at the beach. The Beach Boys played over a state-of-the-art jukebox, perfect for the SoCal vibe.

Knox tended bar and Luke smiled to himself, watching as his younger brother leaned across the bar, flirting with a busty redhead wearing short-shorts and a tank top. With his dark hair and brown eyes, Knox had no trouble getting the girls. Not that Luke did, either. He just didn't stay in one place long enough to hang on to any of them.

He set his bags against the wall and slid into the seat at the end of the bar.

Knox tore himself away from his redhead and walked over to greet him.

"About time you got here," Knox said, a hint of shadowy pain behind his words.

"I got here as fast as I could."

"Aunt Claire is on her way over. So are Gabe and James. Not sure if Hunter will make it. We'll see who shows up."

"Has everyone been notified?"

"Aunt Claire spoke to everyone but Finn. She had to send him an email. Hell of a way for our baby brother to find out his father is dead, but I guess he's flying off some carrier somewhere in the world. I texted him and emailed him, but I haven't heard back."

He wasn't surprised. Finn was a pilot for the US Navy, and he was not an easy man to reach. But while he might be the youngest, he was probably the toughest one of them all.

"How's James doing?" he asked. It was no secret that of all the Brannigan brothers, James was probably the closest to their dad. "He must be pissed that Dad didn't tell him he was sick—unless he made an exception for James?"

"Not according to Aunt Claire—we were all left out of it. Dad didn't want us to watch him die. I guess that was considerate of him."

"I'm sure he thought so."

"You don't?" Knox challenged.

"I need a drink."

"Me, too," a man said as he slid onto the stool next to him. "You look like shit, Luke."

He tipped his head to his older brother Gabe.

Gabe looked a lot better than he did in dark-gray slacks, a white button-down shirt, and maroon tie. He could always count on Gabe to have things together. He'd been running a very successful real-estate development company the past five years, and today he looked every inch the successful businessman.

"Just got off a plane," he said.

Gabe gave him a half-smile. "You're always getting off a plane, Luke. What can I buy you?"

"I'm buying," Knox interrupted. "And we're not drinking beer tonight." He pulled a bottle out of the glass case behind the bar. "In Dad's honor, we have Bushmills 21 single malt, his favorite."

"Very appropriate," Gabe said, as Knox poured the whiskey into three glasses.

"Who wants to make a toast?" Knox asked.

"You go, Luke," Gabe said.

He swirled the whiskey in his glass as he looked down at the amber liquid. "I can't think of anything I want to say." He paused. "Last time I had this whiskey was on my twenty-first birthday."

"With Dad?" Gabe asked. "He bought me a drink on my twenty-first birthday, too."

He shook his head. "It was supposed to be with Dad. He had invited me to dinner, but business came up. I was already in the restaurant bar waiting for him when I got a call from his assistant that he was sorry but he couldn't make it. I was about to leave when the bartender said my father had told him to buy me a drink—this drink. I had another four after that. I don't remember the rest of the night." He took a swig of the whiskey. It was damn good. Of course, his father wouldn't drink anything but the best.

He set the glass down, realizing his brothers were

looking at him with varying degrees of concern.

"Don't worry, I'm not going to cry," he said dryly. "I'm just exhausted."

"And pissed," Knox commented.

He couldn't argue with that. But he was saved from making further explanations by the arrival of another Brannigan brother, his oldest sibling, James. Like Gabe, James wore dark slacks and a dress shirt and looked like he'd just come from signing one of his many business deals. If anyone could compete with his father, it was James.

"Let's move this conversation to a table," Knox said, motioning the group toward the back of the bar. "I'll get Eban to fill in for me."

Luke settled in at the table with his back against the wall as James, Gabe, and Knox filled the other chairs. Knox set down the bottle of whiskey and started to pour James a glass, but his oldest brother held up his hand.

"None for me," James said.

"Seriously?" Knox asked, raising an eyebrow. "We're toasting to Dad."

"I have work to do later."

"It's one drink," Knox complained.

James shrugged. "It's rarely one drink where you guys are concerned."

"Don't throw me under the bus with these two," Gabe complained.

Luke smiled. He rarely missed home, but he did miss his brothers. He pushed his empty glass across the table. "I'm happy to be on the bus. I'll take another shot."

Knox grinned back at him and poured him some more whiskey. "Dad liked being on the bus, too. He enjoyed his whiskey. One of the few things we had in common."

"I'll drink to that," he said, clinking glasses with Knox. "But what I can't drink to is the fact that Dad kept us all in the dark about his illness and that he's still calling the shots on exactly how we should mourn him. He'd probably hate that we were here together talking about him."

"That's not true, Luke," James said. "Dad would appreciate us getting together. He wanted to protect us from the sadness of his death and the burden of a funeral, but I think he'd like us talking about him. That's why I got on a plane and flew across country to join you."

"So New York is really your home now?" he asked. "I guess you and your expensive suits fit right in there."

"They do, yes," James said. "Speaking of expensive suits and expensive toys…" He turned his attention to Gabe. "Tell me that is not your Aston Martin in the parking lot."

Gabe grinned. "It's all mine."

"I can't believe you spent so much cash on a car," James said.

"It was a gift from a client."

"What exactly do you do for your clients?" Knox joked.

"I make them happy and sometimes they pay me back."

"So you drove down from Silicon Valley?" Luke asked, remembering an email he'd gotten a while back about Gabe moving his operations from LA to Northern California.

"I did. It was a good drive. Gave me a chance to

clear my head."

Luke was happy for Gabe, but his head felt anything but clear. "Getting back to Dad. It doesn't bother any of you that he didn't tell us he was sick? Or maybe he told you, James? You were the closest to him."

"He didn't tell me anything," James replied. "I spoke to him several times in the past month. Only once did he sound tense. When I asked him about it, he said he'd spent the day on his boat, and he was just tired. If he had told me, I would have been with him."

"Well, I'm not surprised that Dad kept his silence," Gabe put in. "Our father always did exactly what he wanted to do. He died the same way. Is it really that shocking?"

Luke glanced at Knox, who hadn't had much to say on the subject. "What do you think?"

Knox shrugged. "The old man has been a mystery to me for most of my life. But it doesn't matter. We can't change anything. It is what it is."

"That's true. Who else is coming tonight? Where's Max?" he asked.

"Who knows?" Knox replied. "He claims he's working in something called protective services, but I'm sure it's black ops, and he's probably in the Middle East."

He nodded. Max had been a Navy SEAL, and what he'd been doing since getting out of the service seemed open for interpretation. With Finn on a carrier, that left Hunter.

"What about Hunter?" He directed his question to Gabe. Hunter and Gabe were twins and had always been their own close unit in a sea of Brannigan brothers.

"I texted him last night," Gabe replied. "He's also out of the country; he doesn't know when he'll be back."

"We need to find a time when we can all get together," James said. "No official memorial service, but all seven of us in one room would be good."

"Good luck with that," Luke said. "I can't remember the last time that happened." As he finished speaking, his aunt came over to the table.

Claire was his mother's younger sister. She'd always been a bohemian and a free spirit. She'd been married twice, with a daughter from each marriage. She was now single and spent most of her days painting and managing a small art gallery in Venice Beach.

Today she was dressed in a flowing, gauzy dress, with an abundance of silver bangles, a couple of rings and big hoop earrings. She had dark-brown hair and brown eyes that almost always held a sparkle, but today that sparkle had dimmed.

"Well, well, if this isn't a handsome group," she said.

James got up and offered her his chair, then pulled over one from a nearby table. "Have a seat, Aunt Claire."

"Thanks, honey," she said. "It's so nice to see all of you. Laurel and Hannah wanted to come, but I thought you might need this night to be by yourselves."

"How are Laurel and Hannah doing?" Luke asked. He was interested in his cousins, but he was even more interested in postponing whatever Claire had come to the bar to tell them.

"They're well. Laurel is playing her violin with

the Los Angeles Philharmonic, and Hannah is waiting tables at the Beachside Bistro while going to culinary school at night." She paused. "Are we waiting for anyone else?"

"It's just us," Knox said.

"Well, I'm glad at least some of you could come. I'll get right to it. As I told all of you, your father had very specific wishes about the way he wanted to die and about the distribution of his estate, which, as you know, is quite large." She paused. "There are a lot of details that you'll be hearing more about from your father's lawyer, but I guess the main thing you need to know is that the bulk of the estate will be distributed in five years."

"Five years?" James asked with a frown. "Why so long?"

"Your father told me that he was proud of how you were all your own men, and he wanted that to continue for a while longer."

"That's ridiculous," James said tersely. "He didn't think he could trust us with his money? We've each been our own men for more than a decade."

Claire gave James a compassionate smile. "I know that; I'm just telling you the facts. Your father's attorney, as well as several other trustees, will manage the financials over the next five years. They'll be reporting to all of you on a quarterly basis. I'm sure you have a lot of questions, and heaven knows your father amassed a great deal of money, property, and other assets over his lifetime. But in the meantime, your dad left each of you a personal legacy. And before you ask me what it is, I can say quite frankly that I don't know. He said he was giving you each something that he thought would bring value to your lives. He gave me an envelope with each of your names on it. I don't know what's inside." She opened her large handbag and handed envelopes to Knox, James, and Luke.

"What about Gabe?" Luke asked.

Claire met Gabe's gaze across the table, then looked at Luke. "I already gave Gabe his legacy. We met earlier today."

"Why is that?" Luke asked curiously.

For the first time all night, Gabe looked uneasy. He sat back in his chair, folding his arms across his chest. "We met earlier because I wasn't sure I could make this meeting. But it turned out I could."

"What did you get from Dad?" Luke asked.

"The ranch in Calabasas," Gabe replied.

"Dad gave you the family ranch?" Knox asked, surprise in his voice.

"Yes, but there are strings attached. We are talking about Dad, after all," Gabe said.

"What strings?" James asked.

"Yeah, what strings?" Luke put in.

"I don't want to talk about it right now," Gabe said. "Let's see what the rest of you got."

"What do you mean you don't want to talk about it?" James asked. "You inherit the family home, and you don't want to discuss it?"

"Look, I didn't ask for it," Gabe said. "And it wasn't the generous gift you think it is."

"Don't be so cryptic," Luke said. "Spit it out."

"Another time," Gabe said tersely. "Why don't the rest of you open your envelopes? James, you should start."

James opened his envelope and pulled out a piece of paper. "It's a deed," he said, his gaze narrowing as he read the words on the page.

"To what?" Luke asked impatiently.

"The Villa Pietro Winery on the Amalfi Coast of Italy," James murmured. "What the hell is this?"

"Dad owned a winery?" Knox asked.

"First I heard about it," James said.

Luke shook his head at Knox's enquiring look and glanced at Gabe, who also seemed baffled.

"I can't believe he left you a winery," Knox told James. "I'm the one in the bar business."

"I would hardly call bartending being in the business," James said sharply.

"And I wouldn't call giving a winery to someone who doesn't appreciate a good wine a very smart business decision," Knox retorted.

The ring of James's phone interrupted their conversation. James read a text, then said, "I have to go. I need to take care of some business."

"You're leaving now?" Luke asked. "You don't want to know what Knox and I got?"

"You can tell me later. Sorry, I have to take care of something." James got to his feet and looked at Luke. "Are you staying in town? Can we meet tomorrow?"

"No idea," he muttered. "I need to get some sleep at some point."

"Well, keep in touch."

"Sure thing."

"I'm going to leave, too," Claire said, standing up. "I'm around if any of you want to talk." She paused. "Your dad told me that he remembered how difficult it was on all of you when your mom died. He felt so helpless to comfort you. Those days after the accident when your mom lingered in the hospital caught between life and death were the hardest days of his life." Her eyes blurred with tears. "He didn't want you to have to go through that again with him. He didn't want any good-byes. He wanted you to remember him as he lived, the times you shared together. I know it's hard to understand it, but what he did—he did out of love." She gave them a sad smile. "I'm always going to be here for you boys. You know that, I hope. I love you as if you were my own. So don't be strangers, okay?"

"Okay," Luke said, getting up to give her a hug. His brothers followed.

After his aunt and James left, it was just the three of them.

"Well," Gabe said, giving them both an expectant look. "What did you guys get from Dad?"

"You go first," he said to Knox, wanting to postpone his legacy as long as possible.

Knox opened up his envelope and pulled out a key. "What does this go to?" He frowned as he turned the key over in his hand. Then he looked back into the envelope and pulled out a piece of paper. "This is an address. Maybe it's a key to a storage locker. I guess I'm not going to find out what I have tonight." He tipped his head to Luke. "Your turn."

He slid his finger under the flap of the envelope and pulled out a piece of paper. It was also a property deed. It took him a moment to realize what it was. "The Algoma Resort in Yosemite Valley," he muttered. "He gave me the mountain lodge where he and Mom met. This is crazy. Why would he think I would want a resort?"

"I don't think these legacies are about anything we want but what Dad thinks we need," Gabe said.

"Well, I don't need a lodge," he said firmly. The last thing he wanted was roots. But then, his dad had never understood him in life; why should death be any different?

He slipped the deed back into the envelope and pushed his empty glass across the table. "I'll take another drink."

Two

Luke battled jet lag and a killer hangover on his drive to the Algoma Resort just outside of Yosemite National Park on Wednesday morning. He could have waited a few days or weeks or even months to check out his legacy, but during a long night of tossing and turning, he'd decided that getting out of town was just what he needed.

It had felt strange to be in Los Angeles, the city where his father had truly been a king among men, knowing that he was gone. The press was just catching wind of his dad's death, and in the days to come there would be paparazzi everywhere. Colin Brannigan had been a very wealthy man, with a long list of businesses and properties including a movie studio, a talent agency, a hotel and a dozen other homes around the world. It would probably take five years for the lawyers just to figure out how to disperse everything.

He wasn't that pissed off about having to wait for the estate to be settled. He'd never wanted his dad's money. He'd always wanted to make it on his own. Not that some extra cash wouldn't help finance a bigger budget for his next film, but he'd get there with or without his dad's help. In fact, he might get there faster if he sold the resort, which seemed like the obvious thing to do.

He didn't know why his dad had given it to him. He wasn't a landowner or a property manager; he was an adventurer. He lived his life out of a backpack and a duffel bag. He traveled light; he didn't know any other way to do it.

Turning up the radio, he tried to drown out his thoughts with some classic rock. He wished he had another trip to make, but the base jumping in Norway had been the last piece of his film. Now it was on to editing and production, then distribution and release, and most of that work would take place in LA. The next project was only in the planning stages, so if there was a good time to make this trip, it was probably now.

He actually loved Yosemite, with its majestic mountain peaks, lush forested valley, and spectacular waterfalls. Algoma was a Native American word that meant *Valley of Flowers*, and as he got closer to his destination, those flowers bloomed in abundance.

Everything about this part of California was spectacular. Yosemite National Park covered the western slopes of the Sierra Nevada Mountain Range and offered some of the ultimate experiences in rock and mountain climbing.

He'd climbed the sheer rock cliffs of El Capitan and Half Dome before his twenty-fifth birthday. But he hadn't stayed at the Algoma Resort on those trips. He'd either slept in a tent tied to the side of the cliff face or in a cabin in the valley. The last time he'd been to the resort he'd been seven years old. It was the last family trip they'd made five months before his mom died. They'd never gone back after that.

The family had splintered apart without his mother's steadying influence. His dad had hired nannies by the dozen to watch him and his six brothers, but while his father had provided for all their material needs, he hadn't been around much. His dad had once told him that he'd been so caught up in his own grief that he hadn't known what to do, hadn't understood how to be a father without his wife at his side, but that he'd done his best.

His best hadn't been all that good.

But it was what it was. As Gabe had said, his dad always lived life on his terms. Colin Brannigan was the sun, and everyone else moved around him.

Luke was going to miss that sun, even though he hadn't been warmed by it all that often. He grabbed for the coffee he'd picked up twenty minutes earlier. It was starting to chill, but it still gave him the caffeine jolt he needed.

As he sipped his coffee, he wondered about the legacies his brothers had received. He was surprised Gabe had gotten the family home—not that Gabe seemed that happy about it—and Luke was really curious about the strings his father had added to that legacy, but Gabe would only talk when he wanted to talk. Since Gabe worked in real-estate, perhaps it made sense. Although he would have thought James would have been a better choice. As the oldest sibling, James seemed the one most likely to carry on the family traditions.

He smiled to himself at that thought. What family

traditions? The only tradition they had was every man for himself. Not exactly a bonding family mantra.

And James hadn't gotten anything tied to the family. He'd received a deed to a winery in Italy—a winery none of them had ever heard of. Apparently, their father had had more than one secret.

He was also curious about what Knox's key opened. He'd left before Knox had had a chance to go down to the storage unit. Maybe it was a car or a boat. Luke wouldn't have minded getting the speedboat or the Porsche, but apparently his love of the outdoors had gotten him a mountain resort. He didn't even know his father had bought the place. When had that happened? And why had his father bought a place he had no intention of ever going to again?

Was it out of nostalgia? Sentiment? It certainly didn't seem like the best business proposition. On the other hand, his father hadn't amassed a fortune by buying things for sentimental reasons, so maybe he had had a different motive.

He straightened in his seat as he saw the sign for the resort. He drove under an iron archway and down a long, winding, one-lane, barely-paved road that felt like it was taking him back in time.

The years in between visits peeled away. He remembered being in a mini-van with his mom and a couple of his brothers when they'd come to the resort for that last summer vacation.

They'd been such a big family they'd had to take two cars to the camp. He'd been with his mom, Gabe, Knox, and Finn, while his dad had taken James, Max and Hunter with him. He'd been happy to go with his mom. She liked to sing along to songs on the radio, and he'd liked the sound of her voice. She wasn't a particularly good singer, but she sang with enthusiasm, and it always made him happy.

His gut tightened as the memory flew through his head. It was strange the things that he remembered about her, random moments in time. Some were so fleeting they were difficult to hang on to. He wondered if eventually they'd all just disappear. He hoped not, but the further he got from age seven, the harder it was to remember the details.

Glancing out the window, he saw horses grazing in the meadows, a dozen or so weathered cabins set along the river, a boat dock for fishing trips and river rafting, an archery range in a wide meadow, and the barbecue and picnic area under the tall, towering ponderosa pines and white fir trees. More memories ran through his head.

That last vacation had been filled with firsts for him: the first time he'd ridden a horse, the first time he'd gone rafting, the first time he'd climbed a rock wall. It was that experience that had started his love affair with the outdoors, with towering mountains and rushing rapids, with the excitement and adrenaline rush that came from challenging himself.

Funny—he hadn't realized his passion had started here. Actually, he hadn't really thought about it, but now it seemed so clear.

Eventually, the road came to an end, turning into a parking lot next to the lodge.

He took the nearest spot, then got out and looked around.

The three-story manor house with a huge wraparound porch was the centerpiece of the resort. As he recalled, the lodge had nine or ten bedrooms; the rest of the visitors stayed in the cabins along the river. Inside the lodge was a living room, a dining room, a library, and a game room. He remembered hours spent playing Ping-Pong and pinball with his brothers while his parents had drunk wine and talked to other adults in the living room.

Glancing to the right of the lodge, he saw the paved path leading to the pool area. Brightly colored umbrellas hung over patio tables that curved in a circle around the pool and the hot tub. He could hear a couple of kids yelling *Marco Polo* to each other, and he smiled to himself, thinking some things never changed.

Across from the house was the stable area with a big barn and two rings for horseback riding lessons. A couple stood by the smaller ring, watching their young daughter take a lesson. The white-haired man giving instructions looked familiar. Maybe it was the same guy who'd put him on a horse when he was seven.

Shaking his head at all the memories, Luke walked out of the parking lot, heading toward the house. He was about ten feet away when a woman came through the front door and down the steps. She wore skinny white jeans and a yellow tank top. A pile of wavy blonde hair fell around her shoulders.

His heart came to a crashing halt. His breath froze in his chest. The pretty blonde took him back to another time. He wasn't seven years old in this new memory; he was twenty and madly in love with his college girlfriend, a woman he hadn't seen in almost a decade, a woman with whom he'd had the worst breakup of his life—Lizzie Parker.

Lizzie stopped abruptly, her eyes widening in recognition as her gaze ran down his body. And not for the first time, he wished he didn't have a killer headache, a bad hangover, and a serious case of jet lag, because seeing Lizzie again had put him into a serious head-spin. If the car were a little closer, he might have leaned against it or jumped inside and headed back the way he'd come.

"Luke," she said, putting a hand to her heart. "Is it really you?"

He nodded, not quite able to get any words out.

She took a tentative step forward, then stopped.

He did the same. They were closer, but there was still distance between them. Finally, he found his voice. "What are you doing here, Lizzie?"

"What do you mean?" she asked, more surprise in her voice. "You don't know?"

"Know what?"

"I'm the manager."

"What?" It didn't make sense that she was the manager. Lizzie was a concert pianist, not a hotel manager.

"Your dad gave me the job six months ago."

"My dad gave you the job," he echoed in confusion. "I don't understand."

"He didn't tell you?" She answered her own question. "Of course he didn't tell you. He probably didn't know where to find you. Well, if you have a problem with it, you should take it up with him."

"Take it up with him?" he repeated, feeling like a dimwit. "How the hell am I supposed to do that?"

"Just call him. I know you don't get along that well. He told me he never sees you, and that he feels badly about it. I know he wasn't the perfect dad, but if you tried to reach out a little, he would probably meet you halfway—"

He cut her off with a shake of his head, unable to

hear one more word about his father. "He's dead, Lizzie. My dad is dead." His words drained the blood from her face.

She swayed a little, and he had to fight back a very old instinct to rush to her, to protect her, to save her. But that wasn't his job anymore; it hadn't been for a very long time.

"That's impossible," she said slowly. "I talked to him a week ago. He sounded a little tired, but he didn't say anything was wrong. What happened? Was it an accident?"

"No. He apparently died of cancer several days ago."

"I had no idea," she murmured.

"No one did. Dad didn't tell anyone in the family that he had been diagnosed a month earlier. No one knew he was sick. No one knew he died. He was staying at his house in the Bahamas. He was secluded, surrounded only by people he paid to take care of him."

"I can't believe it," she murmured, her gaze softening as it came back to rest on his. "I'm sorry, Luke."

He didn't want her sympathy. He didn't want his father to be dead. He didn't want this resort, but somehow he'd ended up with all three.

They stared at each other for at least a minute. "I still don't understand what you're doing here," he said finally. "You're a musician. Now you're running a lodge?"

"Sometimes life doesn't turn out the way you think." She crossed her arms in front of her chest.

The move brought his gaze to her beautiful breasts. It had been a long time, but he could still remember kissing every inch of her body. He could still hear her urgent pleas in his ear: *don't stop, Luke, don't ever stop.*

He sucked in a breath, looking back into her face, but that didn't help. She was even prettier than he remembered with her blue eyes the color of a morning sky, her skin reddened by the sun, her lips sweet and full. She'd filled out a bit since he'd last seen her; she was still slender, but not teenage-thin. And her eyes held a few more shadows. He'd put some of them there, but he wondered where the others had come from.

"Are you here by yourself?" Lizzie asked.

"Do you see anyone else?"

She shrugged. "Are you staying? You didn't make a reservation."

"Do you have a room?" he countered.

"One of the smaller cabins is available, but the lodge is sold out through Labor Day weekend."

"I'll take whatever you have."

"For one night?"

"Not sure."

"Okay," she said, her tone cautious and careful. "Do you need help with your bags?"

"I can get my own bags."

"Then I'll see you inside."

"Great." He blew out a breath as she returned to the house. He'd come here with one big question: Why had his dad left him the resort?

Now, he had more questions: Why was Lizzie here? Why had his father hired her without telling him? And why on earth had he decided to spend the night?

Unfortunately, he didn't have any answers…

Lizzie walked across the lobby to the tall reception desk and stepped behind it, putting a hand on the counter to steady herself. She couldn't believe Luke was here. She also couldn't believe Colin Brannigan was dead. If anyone had told her an hour ago that either of those things would be true, she wouldn't have believed them.

The two Brannigan men had impacted her life in huge and very different ways.

Luke had broken her heart when she was twenty.

Six months ago, Colin had been her savior—an unexpected white knight who had appeared during the worst moment of her life.

Now, Colin was gone and Luke was here. Both events seemed incredible.

The front door opened and Luke walked in, a backpack over his shoulders, a duffel bag in his hand. She wished he'd gotten fat or gone bald, instead of looking hunky and hot in faded jeans and a T-shirt that clung to his chest and ripped abs. He'd always been in great shape, and that hadn't changed.

But he looked a little worse for wear today: his dark-brown eyes were bloodshot, his beard was on the scruffy side, and there was an air of weariness about him. She had a feeling his dad's death had affected him more than he would admit. The two of them had had a very complicated relationship.

Clearing her throat, she threw back her shoulders and got down to business. She didn't know why Luke was here. It had to have something to do with his dad's death. Surely he wouldn't stay long, probably no more than a night. Then things would go back to normal, although in recent months she'd discovered that *normal* was a constantly changing state.

Now that Colin was dead, there could be big changes coming to the resort. The best-case scenario was that she would continue to manage the resort, and deal with Colin's lawyers as she'd been doing the past six months. But somehow Luke's appearance didn't bode well for a best-case scenario.

Turning to her computer, she put in a reservation for the only available cabin, wishing she had something better to give Luke, but she didn't.

She grabbed a key from under the desk and pushed it across the counter. "You'll be in Cabin Eleven. If you go back down the road, it's the last cabin on the right. You can park in front. It has a nice view of the river."

He took the key. "Thanks."

"Are you planning to go to Yosemite? Are you scouting the area for one of your films?"

"No."

She was a little surprised at how reticent he was. He'd always been a man of strong opinions, of action, a man who knew what he wanted and went after it with single-minded purpose. He seemed bemused and confused today, probably because of his father's death. She could understand that feeling. But she needed some answers. "What are you doing here, Luke?"

"My father left me this resort, Liz."

She swallowed hard at that piece of information. "Really? Just you?"

"Yeah. Just me. I only found out about it last night. I needed to get out of LA to clear my head, so I figured I'd come up here and see what was what. I sure didn't expect to find you here, Lizzie." He paused. "You said my dad gave you the job. How did that happen?"

"Your cousin Laurel. She and I have kept in touch over the years. We played for the same orchestra for a few months. Anyway, she told her mom that I needed a job and a place to live, and Claire talked to your father, and I ended up here."

He frowned as he gazed back at her. "That sounds like a very short version of a much longer story."

He was right, but she didn't really want to get into a longer explanation. "It's all that matters. I've been managing the place for the last six months, and bookings are up. I've done a good job, and I can keep doing a good job." She infused as much confidence into her statement as she could, but the idea of Luke being her boss was a little hard to stomach. How on earth could that work?

"I doubt I'll keep the property," he said. "I don't know anything about running a resort, and I'm not particularly interested in being an owner. I'll probably put everything up for sale."

Her heart sank at that piece of information. "You might want to think about that. The resort could bring in some good income." As soon as she finished speaking, she realized how stupid she'd just sounded. "But then you probably don't need cash. Your dad must have left you a lot more than this resort."

"Not exactly," he said cryptically.

"Well, you should still think about things. You may not know anything about running a resort, but I do. You could be a silent owner, much the way your father was. You could just let things run, not worry about the details."

He tapped his key against the counter, his brown-eyed gaze narrowing on her. "I don't get it, Liz. I don't understand why you're here, why you're running this lodge. It's the last job I'd expect to find you in."

Before she could explain, *her reason for being here* came sauntering into the lobby wearing a pair of white denim shorts that barely covered her ass and a skimpy top. Her brown hair was tinged with purple and pink, and she had a phone in her hand and headphones in her ears.

She'd been trying to get Kaitlyn downstairs for the past two hours. Of course, she would have to make her appearance now.

Kaitlyn stopped and gave Liz a bored look, although that look changed when her gaze moved to Luke.

She straightened a little, then pulled the headphones out of her ears and said, "Why are you blowing up my phone with a million texts?"

"Because I could use your help," she replied. "You're supposed to be helping Shari make cookies for the children's workshop at two."

"Why can't she do it herself? You pay her to cook."

"And I'll pay you, too, if you actually work."

Kaitlyn looked down at her phone and then started texting.

Lizzie sighed, knowing that the texting wasn't just to keep up with her friends, it was to annoy her.

"Kaitlyn," she said sharply. "Shari is waiting."

"Yeah, yeah, yeah." Kaitlyn looked at Luke. "Are you staying here?"

"I am," Luke replied.

"Do you need help with your bags?" she asked.

"No, he doesn't," she answered for Luke, seeing

Kaitlyn's very inappropriate thirteen-year-old flirtatious smile. "This is Luke Brannigan. His father owns the resort."

"Actually, I own it now," Luke said.

Liz ignored that. "This is my niece, Kaitlyn Allen."

"So you're Aunt Lizzie's boss now?" Kaitlyn asked with interest. "Because I have a few complaints."

Luke smiled. "I have a feeling your aunt has some complaints, too."

Kaitlyn shrugged, stuck her headphones back in her ears and sauntered toward the kitchen.

"I can't believe Kaitlyn is a teenager," Luke murmured. "Last time I saw her, she was three. Are your sister and brother-in-law here, too?"

"No." Her stomach twisted with pain. "They're not here." She took a breath for strength. "They were killed in a car crash while they were vacationing in Hawaii six months ago. As you might remember, my mom has a lot of issues that make it impossible for her to take Kaitlyn in, so it was up to me to do it."

Sympathy entered his eyes. "Damn. I'm sorry, Lizzie."

"So that's why I needed a new job and a place to live. Your father was a lifesaver. I don't know what I would have done without his help."

"I had no idea." He ran a hand through his hair. "That's rough. Kelly was great, and Brian was a good guy, too."

"It's been really hard, but we're doing okay."

"Are you? Kaitlyn seems like a handful."

"She's having a difficult time," she conceded. "I can't blame her. Her entire world was shattered. I'm just hoping that being here in the mountains will be good for her. She would have rather stayed in LA, but it wasn't a good environment for her in her present angry and rebellious mood." She took a breath. "I am a little worried about what's going to happen now that you're here." A gleam sparked in his eyes, and she realized her choice of words had taken him down the wrong path. "Not personally—professionally," she said quickly. "I don't want to lose my job. I hope you'll give me a chance to show you that the resort could be a good investment for you."

"I'm not really about investments, Lizzie."

"There are other benefits. Look where you are— Yosemite Valley—one of the most beautiful places on earth. And it has all your favorite things: rock climbing, rafting, camping…you might want to keep it. You might want to stay here sometimes when you're not on the road."

"That's almost never."

"Then it won't really be a burden for you. Things can keep going just the way they have been the past six months. I can work through your dad's lawyers. I can send you reports in email. You don't have to come here, live here, or even talk to me." Her pitch sounded a little desperate, but she didn't have time to come up with a better argument. She had the sense that Luke wasn't going to stay here long enough to see how much more potential the resort had. And maybe he wouldn't want to help her because of their past.

Luke cleared his throat. "I need to think."

She was a little surprised by his response. The Luke she knew acted first and thought about it later. Maybe he'd changed—hopefully in a good way. "Okay. You should think. And you should spend some time here, get to know the place. We start serving lunch in ten minutes if you're hungry."

"I am hungry," he said, as if happy he could make that one decision. "I'm going to stash my things, and then I'll be back."

"Great," she said, forcing a smile.

As soon as he left, her smile faded. She'd really thought the worst was over for a while. She'd been wrong about that.

Well, she wasn't going down without a fight, because this wasn't just about her future; it was also about Kaitlyn's.

She just wished Colin had left the resort to one of his other sons. She could have dealt far more easily with Knox or Gabe or any of Luke's other brothers. But it had to be Luke. And knowing Colin, she had a feeling that was not at all a coincidence.

Three

The dining room was about a quarter-full when Luke made his way to the lodge for lunch. The room was warm and inviting, with dark paneled walls, exposed beams, hardwood floors, and round tables decorated with small glass vases filled with wildflowers. The sight of those flowers brought a wave of pain.

Lizzie had always loved wildflowers. She was not the girl who wanted perfect roses or rare orchids; she liked flowers that grew among the weeds. She thought they were tough and resilient, kind of like her.

Lizzie had not had an easy childhood. Her father had abandoned the family when she was three. Her mother had struggled to raise her and her sister Kelly, battling depression and working long hours to try to take care of the girls. Lizzie had worked hard, too. Her college scholarship hadn't covered all of her expenses, so she'd gotten a job in the dining hall on campus, serving up bean and beef burritos.

He smiled to himself, thinking about all those

bean and beef burritos he'd eaten just so he could see her for a few minutes in the middle of the day.

Now, she'd lost her sister and brother-in-law and had taken on the raising of a sullen teenage girl. Running a mountain lodge was a far cry from being a concert pianist, the dream she'd had all of her life. He couldn't quite believe she'd given it all up. On the other hand, it didn't sound as if she'd had another choice.

Lizzie came over, giving him a wary look. "You can sit anywhere you like." She handed him a menu. "Our chef makes a few specials every day. Everything is good."

He took the menu out of her hand and looked around the room. Three of the tables were filled but there was an open table by the window. He made his way over to that one. As he looked at the menu, he noted the hearty but healthy offerings: turkey chili with kale salad, roasted chicken and organic vegetables, grilled salmon and quinoa.

Lizzie had told him everything was good and right now everything looked good to him. When a young guy came over to take his order, he settled on the roasted chicken and added a cup of clam chowder to start.

While he was waiting for his food, he glanced over at Lizzie, who was chatting with one of the guests, giving them tips on which hiking trail to take.

She glanced away from her conversation for a brief moment, catching his eye, her gaze clinging to his for a long moment.

A warmth spread through him. He'd felt numb since hearing of his father's death, but now he felt anticipation and shockingly, a little fear.

He'd always thought Lizzie could change his life; it was one of the reasons they'd broken up. He hadn't wanted her to change his life, and she hadn't wanted him to change hers. He'd actually thought that they might never see each other again—that maybe they had to be apart in order to get what they both wanted.

But here they were—together again.

His father had known Lizzie was here, and now he knew why he'd been left the resort. His dad had always liked Lizzie; he'd thought she was good for him. In fact, when they'd broken up, his dad had told him he was a fool to let her go and that someday he'd be sorry.

That was Colin. Saying what he thought without a filter, without a care for how blunt or hurtful he might be. His father had always liked to speak the truth, but sometimes the truth was painful.

He didn't know if he'd been a fool to let her go. But he did know that he'd missed her, never more so than at this moment. He was happy when the waiter stepped between him and Lizzie to set down his meal.

He ate with enthusiasm, the creamy flavor of the clam chowder comforting and warming, the roasted chicken flavorful and energizing. He felt like he hadn't eaten in days, and for the first time since he'd gotten the news of his dad's death, he was actually hungry, which was a good thing. He was going to need strength to deal with Lizzie. He'd seen the light of battle in her eyes when he'd mentioned selling the resort, and he knew what that look meant. She wasn't going to give up without a fight.

He just had to figure out what he wanted to fight for. He knew next to nothing about the resort. Before he made any decisions, he needed to find out exactly what value the property held and whether it was worth keeping. There had been so few things in his life that he'd ever wanted to keep; he couldn't quite imagine coming to that decision. But if Lizzie wanted a chance to change his mind, he'd give her that.

He hadn't been ready to see her again, but he was even less ready to say good-bye—for the second time.

Lizzie dropped a thick file folder onto the table as Luke finished his lunch.

He wiped his mouth with a napkin. "What's that?"

She slid into the chair across from him. "Accounting reports from the last six months. You'll see that since I got the job, profits have gone up."

He didn't bother to open the file. "You know, I'm not a numbers guy."

"I can summarize things for you. If you're the new owner of the lodge, then you should know how things are going."

"Or I could just sell the place."

"I'm sure that would be the easiest thing for you. You're very good at leaving and not looking back."

There was an edge to her voice and anger in her eyes now. "I thought we weren't making this personal, Lizzie. Do you really want to talk about the past? Because I don't think you're going to come out all that well."

"That's the last thing I want to talk about," she said quickly. "I'm only concerned about the present and the future. Some of us have responsibilities." She blew out a breath. "Why did your father have to leave the resort to you?"

"I suspect it has something to do with you, but I can't ask him."

Her anger dimmed at the reminder. "I am sorry about your dad. He was one of a kind. He wasn't always the best man, but he was always true to himself."

"He was definitely that," he agreed.

"He told me that you two hadn't seen each other much the last few years."

"You talked to him about me?"

"Only briefly. He said he missed you more than you'd probably believe."

"Yeah, right." He didn't believe that for one second.

"And that in some ways, you were the most like him of all of his sons," she added.

"That's not true at all. If anyone is like him, it's James, or maybe Gabe. They like wearing suits and ties and making lots of money."

"Most people do—at least, the making money part." She paused. "Look, I know that I probably can't make a case that will change your mind, but at least spend a few days here. You might like it. We're now offering several adventure packages. We have guides to take guests into the mountains on rock climbing and hiking expeditions. We have a dozen horseback riding trails through some of the prettiest countryside in the world. There's river rafting and a new zip line course a few miles down the road. You like all that stuff. You could have fun here."

"You sound like a brochure. And I can't believe you would put in a zip line course. You don't like heights."

"There are a lot of things I don't like that I have

to deal with," she said sharply. "And it doesn't matter what I like; it's about what will sell, what will bring people to the resort and keep them coming back. I have a lot of ideas that I still want to implement. I just need a little time."

She licked her lips in an anxious manner that once again sent a wave of emotion and reckless desire through him. He had to fight the urge to lean across the table and kiss her concerns away like he'd done so many times before.

"You shouldn't make a decision this big too fast," she added. "You're grieving. You're shocked. Look through the financials. Talk to the accountants. Get some advice. And most of all, spend some time here."

"I suppose I could take a few days," he conceded, although he suspected that even one more day with Lizzie was probably one too many.

"Good," she said, relief filling her blue eyes. "The first thing you should do is see the property. I can take you out this afternoon if you're up for it."

"All right. Let's go now," he said, tossing his napkin onto the table.

For a moment, panic filled her eyes. "Right now?"

"Why not?"

"No reason. You're right. Now is good. I'll meet you out front in twenty minutes. I need to make sure Tina can cover the front desk while we're gone." She pushed the file folder toward him. "Take this with you. You'll want to read it later."

He doubted he'd ever want to read it, but he took the file with him as he left the dining room.

⇒⇒⇐⇐

Liz didn't know why she felt nervous, but as she walked out front to meet Luke twenty minutes later, her palms were sweating and her pulse was racing too fast. She should not be having such a strong reaction to a man who had hurt her deeply, a man she'd already cried far too many tears over, a man who should have stayed in her past.

She had enough on her plate without adding Luke into the mix, but she didn't have a choice. If she wanted to keep her job and her home, she had to convince Luke to hang on to the resort. Once he made a decision to keep the property, he could let his lawyers or accountants deal with her. They wouldn't have to spend time together or talk to each other. He could continue to wander the world, and she could live her life. It could work.

She just had to convince him of that fact.

Luke came down the road from his cabin with the attractive, confident swagger that always got to her. How many times in college had she waited for him just like this? How many times had he grabbed her, kissed the breath out of her, and given her that sexy smile as he said, *Hey, babe, I missed you,* when he'd seen her only hours before?

She drew in a breath, telling herself to get out of the past. But it was difficult to look away when everything about him was so compelling, when her body wanted to remember his touch, his taste, his kiss, even as her brain told her to put the walls up, protect herself.

This was Luke. She'd hurt him. He'd hurt her. None of that could happen again.

Luke looked like he'd just stepped out of the shower. He'd changed into a clean pair of jeans and a navy T-shirt, and his beard was neatly trimmed. He had more energy now. She hoped that was a positive sign. Maybe if he wasn't so dogged with grief and sadness and probably anger, she could appeal to his common sense, business side.

She almost smiled at the thought of Luke having a business side. The last thing he'd ever wanted to do was business. He'd rejected every opportunity his father had thrown at him and swore he'd never wear a suit and tie or go to a nine-to-five job. So far, he'd kept that promise, at least from what she knew about him, which was probably more than she should know. But Luke was a Brannigan, and Brannigan adventures were often reported in the press, especially when the Brannigan was as sexy and single as Luke was. She knew his movies featuring extreme sports had done very well; she just hadn't watched any of them. It was one thing to catch a glimpse of a random photo of Luke and another to watch him on film, talking, laughing, hiking, risking his life…

"I'm ready," he said, interrupting her rambling thoughts. "Are we walking, driving, or riding?"

"Riding, but not one of the horses." She pointed to the nearby golf cart. "That will get us everywhere we want to go."

"Everywhere?" he challenged. "I've found that the places most worth seeing are usually hard to get to."

"Well, we're not climbing any mountains today."

"Too bad. That would probably seal the deal for you."

She waved him toward the golf cart. She was willing to do a lot to hang on to her job, but climbing a mountain wasn't one of them, especially not the way Luke liked to climb, attacking sheer rock cliffs with picks and rope and reckless determination.

She slid behind the wheel of the cart as Luke got into the passenger side. They were a lot closer than she wanted to be. She was suddenly very aware of everything about him: the soapy scent of his skin and the power of his thighs that were so close to hers. She could almost feel the weight of his body on hers, his thighs against her leg, pinning her to the mattress as he made love to her.

Butterflies danced through her stomach, and she drew in a quick breath of mountain air. It was a mistake asking Luke to stay but what choice did she have? She just had to hope she could keep her distance, get his agreement and send him out of town before she could want him again.

Their overwhelming passion for each other had once consumed her, and getting over Luke had been the hardest thing she'd ever done. She couldn't imagine having to go through that a second time.

"How many horses do you have?" Luke asked.

She was surprised that he was interested enough to ask a question. She'd thought this outing would be one long sales pitch for her. "We have eight. Tom Gordon runs the stables. He's been at the resort for almost two decades."

"The white-haired guy?"

She nodded. "That's him."

"I think he gave me a lesson when I was seven."

"You've been here before?" she asked in surprise.

She knew that Colin and his wife had first met at the resort, but Colin hadn't mentioned any trips to the lodge with his family. He'd told her he'd bought the property in honor of his wife when it had gone up for sale two years ago, but once he had the deed in his hands, he couldn't bring himself to go there. It was just too painful.

"A family trip," Luke replied. "It was about five months before my mom died. Dad never brought us back after that."

"It was probably too difficult for him. This place was special because it's where your father met your mother."

"I guess, but he didn't really take us anywhere after she died, and I don't think that's because every spot held painful sentiment."

Hearing the bitterness in his voice, she realized that talking about his father was probably not the way to get Luke on her side. She needed to get him to look at the resort as a good financial investment, not that he cared about that kind of stuff. But he did care about nature and about people living life to the fullest. That's the angle she needed to work. Make him see that the resort provided an opportunity for visitors to have experiences they might not get anywhere else.

The resort was situated near one of the most spectacular parks in the world. Yosemite was a big draw, and their location was even better because they were just outside the park but still close enough to take advantage of all that it had to offer.

She drove under a canopy of trees and then pointed to a nearby meadow where an archery range had been set up. "Archery has been super popular this summer—both kids and adults. There's no one here today, but on the weekends it's hopping."

"I can't imagine anything more boring," he drawled.

It wasn't her thing, either, but she'd seen a lot of her customers enjoy it. "We have other activities, too.

This resort has so much potential, Luke. The previous owners were elderly and running out of money before they finally had to sell to your father, so things got run-down. But we've been making great strides toward bringing everything back to life." She shot him a quick look, but his expression was unreadable, so she continued the tour around the property.

She pointed out the riding trails, the fishing pond, the rock wall for kids, and the acres of open land around the property. She wound her way up one of the nearby foothills, stopping at an overlook to show him the mountains and the river beyond. Then she got out of the cart and walked over to a bench that overlooked a canyon.

Luke followed, his gaze sweeping the view.

"Not bad, huh?" she challenged, certain that there was a part of Luke that would respond to this magnificent vista.

"Not bad," he admitted, digging his hands into his pockets.

"That's El Capitan over there." She pointed to one of Yosemite's most notable mountain peaks.

He nodded. "I've been up there."

"Of course you have. So you know how much this area has to offer. With just a few changes and a little more investment, this resort could be a premier destination vacation for not just families but also thrill seekers."

"You hate thrill seekers. Why would you want to attract them?"

She sighed. "I don't hate thrill seekers, and we are not talking about us, Luke."

"Maybe we should."

He stepped forward, and she had to fight the urge

to step back, but the last thing she wanted was to show any weakness.

"This place is not you, Lizzie," he said, giving her a puzzled look. "Why are you fighting so hard to stay here? I can't imagine you like it that much. You never even wanted to go camping with me. You said there was too much dirt, too many bugs, that nature wasn't your thing."

"That was a long time ago." She paused. "You're right. I wasn't into country getaways before; I was a city girl. But since I've started working here, I've come to appreciate the beauty around me. I thought I would hate all the quiet, but it's comforting after the year I've had. Most importantly, this place is good for Kaitlyn."

"But what about your music? Your career? It meant everything to you. If you couldn't play the piano, you couldn't breathe. Why couldn't you rent a place in LA or some other city and raise Kaitlyn there? Why did you have to come all the way out here?"

"I tried to make Los Angeles work in the beginning. I couldn't keep the house my sister was renting; it was too expensive. But I was able to get a one-bedroom apartment for Kaitlyn and myself. I gave her the bedroom and I slept on the couch. I wanted to keep her in her school and with her friends, but she went wild after the funeral, Luke. She was angry and rebellious and getting into all kinds of trouble. She turned away from her old friends and fell in with a wild crowd. She came home after school one day, and she was drunk and had two new piercings in her ear. I had no idea what to do. Then one of the moms at the school called me and said she saw Kaitlyn smoking with a bunch of older boys outside of a sandwich shop when she was supposed to be at school. She was worried about Kaitlyn, and so was I. That's when I realized I had to make a big move. It was terrifying, but the job up here with a place to stay was the very best alternative."

He gazed back at her. "But you gave up your whole life."

"So I could protect Kaitlyn's. Someday maybe I'll get back to music, but I can't worry about that now. I have bigger problems. Life isn't always about dreams; sometimes it's just about survival. Right now, I'm raising a kid who doesn't like me much and likes her new home even less. But I still think it's the best place for both of us. So that's it. That's my story."

Luke's stare was unreadable and went on far too long.

Finally, she turned away, looking out at the view. Unfortunately, the view reminded her of the last hike they'd taken, the one where Luke had told her that he was leaving school and wanted her to join him for the summer...

She didn't want to think about that day.

"We should go back," she said, turning to face Luke.

"It's like the last time, isn't it?" he asked, either reading her mind or letting the same old memory run through his head. "We climbed to the top of Mount Baldy on the first day of summer between our junior and senior year."

"You talked me into it, and I let you, because I had a feeling you had something big on your mind, and I had to hear it. I think I knew even before you said the words that you were leaving. You were dropping out of college; you were going to travel the world and have adventures."

"And you said you'd go with me, at least for the summer. But you didn't show up at the plane. I waited so long I missed the flight. I called, texted—no answer from you."

She swallowed hard at the reminder. "I couldn't go with you, Luke. I couldn't give up my dream."

"I didn't ask you to give up your dream; I asked you to give me three months. You could have gone back to school in September."

"It wouldn't have been any easier to say good-bye in September, not after a summer together."

"Why didn't you just say that, Lizzie? Why leave me hanging?"

"Because I was young and scared of making the wrong choice. I was afraid if I told you I wasn't going, you'd find a way to talk me into it. It was cowardly not to tell you to your face. I'm not proud of what I did."

"You shouldn't be," he agreed. "You owed me more than that."

"I felt awful after you left, Luke. It hurt so bad. I missed you so much. I almost jumped on a plane to follow you a dozen times."

"But you didn't, and it took you almost three months to answer a text."

"You were so angry with me."

"Hell, yes, I was angry," he said, waving his hand in the air. "You broke us up."

She shook her head. "No, that's not all on me. You broke us up when you decided to leave school. We could have had that summer and another year together. You didn't have to go then. But you wanted to have everything your way. You wanted to travel the world. You wanted to start making films. Did you ever once ask yourself what I might want or need—beyond you? Not playing piano for three months wasn't going to be good for my career."

He gave her a look of disbelief. "You were brilliant. You could have taken off a year and still been better than anyone else. But I wasn't asking for a year, only three months."

"But why did I have to take any time off? Why couldn't you wait?"

"Because I couldn't. School was just a roadblock for me. I wasn't learning anything there."

"Well, I was."

He frowned and let out a heavy sigh.

"Wasn't it easier in the long run that I didn't go with you?" she challenged. "I would have slowed you down. You've been all over the world, jumping out of planes, climbing the highest mountain peaks, challenging the most difficult rapids…" She shook her head. "You would have gotten so frustrated with me. You're afraid of nothing, and I'm afraid of almost everything. We were very different people, Luke. The only thing we did really well together was—" She stopped herself just in time.

A glitter entered his eyes. "At least you can admit that, Lizzie. You could never say you loved me, but you could say you wanted me."

It had always been a bone of contention between them, but admitting love had always been difficult for her. "We need to let the past be the past, Luke. What we had was a decade ago, and we both made mistakes. I can admit that. Can you?"

His lips tightened. "Maybe."

She was actually a little surprised by his answer. "Okay, then. So let's move on."

"I moved on a long time ago."

"I mean—let's move on with this conversation. I'm sure there have been lots of other women in your life."

"Lots," he agreed with a nod.

"Great. Then we don't need to talk about our past anymore." She refused to admit to herself that she felt even the faintest hint of jealousy at the thought of Luke and other women. "Let's focus on the present, on why you're here. I have to admit it still seems surreal."

"To me, too. The last few days have been a bad dream. One minute I'm jumping off a mountain in Norway, and the next my aunt is telling me that my father is dead. And then the lodge and you…it's been a crazy time."

She heard the raw pain in his voice and understood. "I know what it feels like to lose someone you love in a sudden and abrupt manner. When Kelly died, I was confused, angry, and in denial for a while. But I couldn't wallow in emotions. Kaitlyn needed someone to step in and take care of her. She wasn't just emotionally wounded; she also had some minor injuries that needed care."

"Wait. She was in the car with her parents?"

"Yes. She won't talk about it, though. I sent her to a therapist, but she wouldn't open up to her, either. Kaitlyn says she doesn't remember anything. I don't know if it's true, but I know that she's still suffering. I wish she would talk to me. I keep hoping, but there's a wall between us, and I can't seem to tear it down. Every time I ask her anything about her parents or the accident, she clams up. I just hope time will do some healing. Because right now she is one angry kid." She took a deep breath. "I need to keep my job, Luke."

"Look, I get it, Lizzie, but maybe there's a way I can sell the place and stipulate that you have to keep your job here for at least a year."

She supposed that might be better than nothing, but would the new owners be people she could work with? The last thing she needed was more drama.

Thinking for a moment, she realized what she needed to do was show Luke why the resort was important to his dad and why Colin Brannigan had bought it in the first place. Luke might have negative and complicated feelings about his dad, but not when it came to his mother...

"Let's go," she said abruptly. "I need to show you something."

"What's that?"

"A tree."

He raised an eyebrow. "You're going to show me a tree? I'm looking at about a hundred of them right now."

"It's a special tree. Come on."

Four

Liz's special tree on first glance appeared like every other ponderosa pine dotting the slopes of Yosemite Valley. Luke didn't notice anything unique about it until she pointed out the carving of a heart on the trunk with three words scratched out: *Colin loves Kathleen.*

His chest tightened, a knot growing in his throat, as he compulsively traced the line of the heart with his fingers. "How did you know this was here?" he asked, wondering how she'd found this carving among hundreds of trees on the property.

"Your dad told me about it when he hired me. He remembered the exact location even though he hadn't been here in over twenty years."

He shook his head in bemusement, her words just confusing him more. "What exactly did he say?" Even as he asked the question, he wondered why he was dragging it all out. He didn't care, did he?

When it came to any mention of his mother…yes.

He lifted his head to meet Lizzie's gaze. "Tell

me."

"He first met your mother at the creek down there." She pointed to the rocky stream of water about thirty yards away. "Your mother was barefoot, and she was making her way down the creek by jumping from rock to rock. She was wearing cut-off jean shorts and a red tank top, and her blonde hair was up in a ponytail. He said she was the prettiest girl he'd ever seen."

The knot in his throat grew a little bigger. "I can't believe he described her clothes."

Lizzie gave him a sad smile. "He was very specific in his memories of your mother. He said Kathleen was seventeen and he was eighteen when they first met. She was at the lodge with her family, and he was there with friends for a hiking trip after high school graduation. Once he saw her, he forgot all about climbing Half Dome. He sent his friends off without him."

"I can't believe he even contemplated climbing Half Dome. He was not interested in that kind of thing."

"Maybe he was…a long time ago."

He frowned at the idea that his dad had anything in common with him. "Go on."

"They spent every minute of the next four days together. Then she went back to Kentucky, and he went off to college. They tried to do long-distance for a while, but it didn't work, and it was ten years before they ran into each other again in LA. She was twenty-seven and he was twenty-eight then. He said fate put her back in his life and he wasn't going to let her go. They got married the next year, and, well, you know the rest."

He swallowed hard. He'd heard some of the story before—kind of—his aunt had probably told him a version of it, maybe his dad; he couldn't really remember.

"Your dad said that he and your mom used to come back here for vacation," Lizzie added. "It was a special place for them. When he heard that the resort was going under two years ago, he decided to buy it. But after he got the deed, he couldn't bring himself to actually come here without her. He said it would be too hard to visit the places where his beautiful Kathleen had danced from rock to rock, knowing that she would never dance again."

Luke blew out a breath. "Stop," he said, putting up a hand. He felt like his chest might explode if he heard another word. He walked away from Lizzie and stared down at the creek. He could picture his mother there now, the beautiful young woman with the laugh he could never forget. And he could see her dancing across the rocks just the way Lizzie and his father had described.

A moment later, Liz came up next to him. "I'm sorry, Luke. I didn't mean to hurt you."

"You didn't," he said quickly. "I was seven years old when she died; I barely remember her."

"But you remember some things."

"Not as many as I would like."

"I thought your dad might have already told you the story."

"If he did, I don't remember."

"Your father said that your mom brought the light and the heat back into his life, that after his parents died he was very much alone and his world was pretty dark at times. He was very goal-oriented. He chased career and money and power because it gave him something to think about, something he felt he could control."

Her words reminded him that he hadn't thought much about the fact that his dad had lost his parents when he was a teenager. He'd never talked about them, either. Apparently, when the people in his life died, Colin stopped speaking about them. But obviously the fact that his dad had bought this resort meant that he hadn't stopped thinking about his mom.

"He really loved her," Lizzie said.

"There were other women in his life after she died."

She met his gaze. "But he didn't marry any of them."

"Probably didn't want to have to worry about alimony or pre-nups," he said. "Or in the beginning, he couldn't find anyone who wanted a man with seven boys."

"You don't believe that. You're a lot of things, Luke—but cynical isn't one of them. You couldn't do what you do—challenge the world, look for the magnificence—without a core of optimism."

It disturbed him that she still knew things about him no one else knew.

"I've changed," he told her. "I'm not the twenty-year-old kid you used to know."

"I'm not that twenty-year-old girl, either, and maybe that's a good thing. We can handle this situation like adults. Then we can both get what we want."

"What we both want," he mused, as her blue eyes flickered under his gaze. Suddenly what he wanted was extremely clear. He moved forward, putting his hands on her hips, drawing her close.

"Not that," she protested.

"Definitely *that*," he whispered, putting his mouth on hers.

She could not believe Luke was kissing her. Was she dreaming? It certainly felt like it.

Tingles ran down her spine as her mouth opened under his and smoldering desires came rushing back. His kiss was the same and yet it was different. It felt familiar and also new. But, as always, his mouth on hers was a head-spinning and heartbreaking experience.

It had never taken much to go from zero to a hundred miles an hour when it came to Luke. The barest touch had always ignited a firestorm within her and today was no different. In fact, it was worse, because it had been so long, and she'd missed him so much.

She loved the way his mouth took command, the way his tongue danced with hers, the heat that rose between them, the feel of his hands on her body as he pulled her closer, as he refused to let her catch her breath, think, pull away. One impatient, needy, searching kiss followed the next.

She knew she should stop the madness and push him away. No good could come of this. She wasn't crazy about him anymore, was she? She wasn't reckless or impulsive. She couldn't afford to be.

But it felt too good to stop.

Luke reminded her of...the way she used to be. Young, hopeful, passionate, filled with dreams, sure that happiness was just around the corner, and that love would be shared with Luke. They'd met young. It had seemed amazing to have met someone who touched her body and her heart and her soul in such a special way at such a young age.

She'd been so in love with him. He'd promised her the moon and the stars, and she'd promised to be his sun.

And then it had all come crashing down.

That's what she needed to remember—not the happiness but the pain.

She finally pulled away, her heart beating too fast, her blood rushing through her veins, her nerves still clamoring for more.

Luke looked back at her with desire in his intense brown eyes. *He wanted her.*

Her stomach twisted. It wasn't fair that she could still want him, too, after so many years.

She let out a breath and tried to calm herself down. Tucking her hair behind her ears, she was acutely aware of how she could still taste Luke on her lips.

She wanted to look away from him, but she didn't want him to think that she was as bothered as she was. She just wished his gaze would move somewhere else. But that was Luke. He'd always looked right at her. He'd always seen the real her. At least, that's what she'd thought, but in the end, he'd only seen what he needed, not what she needed.

Another breath moved her chest. She had to break the silence. "So…that happened," she said somewhat helplessly.

"Yeah."

"Why did you kiss me, Luke?" It was a foolish

question, but she couldn't stop it from crossing her lips.

"Why did you kiss me back?" he countered.

"You caught me off guard."

"That's not the reason." He paused. "I kissed you, because I've been thinking about it since I saw you come out of the lodge this morning. I wanted to know if it would be the same."

She supposed she'd wanted to know that, too. She waited for him to say it was or it wasn't, but he remained oddly silent. He dug his hands into the pockets of his jeans and rocked back on his heels as his gaze finally moved away from her.

"We should go back," she said. "I have work to do. And you're probably tired from the drive up here."

"In a minute," he replied.

"It always has to be on your terms," she said, irritated that he once again wanted her to jump to his tune, but mostly angry because she still wanted him when she knew she shouldn't.

His gaze swung back to her. "What's wrong?"

"Now you know when something is wrong?" she asked with a touch of sarcasm.

"Yes. I also know when a woman wants me."

"I don't want you," she lied.

"Yes, you do. It didn't go away, Lizzie—what was between us—it's all still there."

She wanted to tell him he was wrong, but she'd never been a good liar. "Maybe for a second," she conceded. "For old times' sake. But we both know where this story ends, so we don't need to keep turning the pages."

His gaze hardened. "I loved you."

"You loved other things more," she said, even

though her heart had skipped a beat at his words. "That's why you left."

"And that's why you stayed."

"See, we're right back where we were."

"Why did it have to be all or nothing, Lizzie? Why couldn't we have done the summer, see where it led?" he asked.

"Because I knew where it would lead. I wanted to get my broken heart out of the way so I could concentrate on school and my career."

"A career you've now thrown away."

"Not thrown away—put away—for a good reason. Plus, I had ten years of music. I played on the biggest stages in the world. I got to do what I dreamed about doing. If it's over now, then it's over. Kaitlyn's life is just beginning. She needs a chance to be all she can be."

"That's very generous."

She shrugged, a little surprised at the compliment; there was so much anger and bitterness between them. "I didn't really have a choice."

"There's always a choice."

"Your life has worked out the way you wanted it to, hasn't it?" she asked. "You don't have any regrets, do you?"

"Mostly not."

"That's good," she said, wondering why it hadn't been an unconditional no. She couldn't help wondering if her absence in his life was the basis of that *mostly*, but that was probably a very egotistical thought. "Are you ready to go yet?"

"I'm ready," he said, falling into step with her as they walked back to the golf cart. Just as they reached the vehicle, he put a hand on her arm. "Lizzie."

"What?" she asked, worried he might kiss her again, and this time she wouldn't have surprise as an excuse.

Conflict moved through his eyes. "Nothing," he said, dropping his hand. "Let's go."

She wanted to feel good about his sudden silence, but she couldn't help wondering what he'd stopped himself from saying.

When they returned to the lodge, she forced a smile on her face and got back to business. As much as she wanted him to go far away, removing any temptation to see what else they still did well together, she still needed to get him to keep the resort. That had to be her focus and nothing else.

"There's a campfire tonight," she said. "Tom will tell the tale of Last Chance Rock; Tina, my assistant manager, plays a mean guitar and has a beautiful voice to entertain the guests; and there will be marshmallows for the kids and wine for the adults. You should come. It's a little hokey, but it's fun. The guests enjoy it, and you can meet some of the other staffers."

"I'll consider it."

"Tomorrow, I can have Tom get you on a horse if you want to try out the trails."

"I'll think about tomorrow—tomorrow."

"One of your favorite lines," she said.

He gave her a small smile. "It's worked for me so far."

"So I'll see you later."

"Most likely."

She hesitated at that cryptic answer. "Just don't leave without saying good-bye, Luke."

"I never just disappear," he said. "That's you,

Lizzie, not me."

She sighed. "We can't get away from that day, can we? I told you why I didn't show up. And I apologized."

"It was a half-ass apology ten years ago and only slightly better now, and that's because you need something from me. Hell of a twist, isn't it?"

"I don't know what you want from me, Luke."

"That's the problem. I don't know, either, Lizzie, but I think we're both going to find out."

———

Luke's cryptic words ran around her head as she entered the lodge. She stopped at the front desk to check with Tina, an attractive twenty-three-year-old who was thrilled to work at the lodge since her boyfriend David worked with Tom at the stables.

"Everything good here?" she asked.

"Quiet today," Tina replied with a happy smile. "Tomorrow will be a different story with everyone checking in for the holiday weekend."

Liz nodded, not at all put out by that thought. She'd enjoyed the busy summer, the constant flow of cash and guests. The fall would be quieter, which would have made it a great time to do some of the cabin remodeling that was needed, but now she didn't know what would happen. Even if Luke agreed to keep the resort, would he want to put more money into it?

"How was your afternoon?" Tina asked, a curious gleam in her eyes. "And who was that gorgeous man you were with?"

"His name is Luke Brannigan."

"He's related to Colin?"

"Yes, he is." She didn't want to discuss Luke or Colin's death just yet. "I do have some news, and I'm sorry if I'm being cryptic, but I want to tell everyone at once. So I'll do it at four o'clock, at our staff meeting."

"Okay, that sounds a little ominous."

"Try not to worry," she said, offering a reassuring smile. "I'm going to check in with Shari. Do you need anything from me right now?"

"Nope, I'm good."

"Great." While Tina didn't need anything, Liz did—a big cup of coffee and a friend to go along with it. She knew where to find both.

When she entered the kitchen, Shari Jordan, the thirty-four-year-old chef, was engaged in massive dinner prep, a pile of chopped tomatoes in front of her, and her knife making quick work of the rest.

"I need coffee," she announced.

"Lucky for you, I just made a pot," Shari replied.

Liz poured herself a mug and took a grateful sip as she leaned against the counter. She watched Shari's skilled knife work for a few moments, in awe of how quickly she could dice tomatoes. She, on the other hand, had never had any talent in the kitchen. Fortunately, she didn't even have to try anymore.

Shari had put her long, dark-red hair into a braid, and she wore an apron over her maternity tank top and stretchy pants. Shari's cheeks were pink from the heated kitchen, or maybe it was from the internal glow that had arrived with her pregnancy eight months earlier.

Shari was married to Brad Jordan, who headed up their adventure programs. They'd been at the resort for six years and had taught Liz a lot about running the place. Fortunately, neither one had wanted her job. Shari only liked being in the kitchen, and Brad had an aversion to paperwork, so it was all good—even better now that they were expecting a baby. Although, she was reminded of the fact they really needed to get a temporary chef in place before the baby came. They only had four weeks to go.

Her mood soured as she thought of what could happen in those four weeks. Forget herself; there were a lot of other people depending on the resort for a job and a place to live should Luke decide to sell.

"So, have you had enough coffee to take the edge off?" Shari asked, looking over at her with a knowing smile. "Because I want to know who Mr. Tall, Dark, and Handsome is and why you felt it necessary to give him a personal tour of the resort when there are a hundred other things to get done before the holiday weekend."

"Who told you?"

"Tina mentioned you went off with a very attractive man."

She took another sip. "Yes. Luke Brannigan. He's one of Colin's sons." While she hadn't wanted to tell the story a dozen times, she needed to talk to her closest friend before she shared the news with the rest of the staff. "I have some bad news, Shari."

"What's that?" Shari asked worriedly.

"Colin died last week. He left the resort to Luke. That's why he's here, and why I gave him a tour. He's not sure what he wants to do with his legacy. He's considering selling out."

Shari set down her knife. "Okay, wait a second, back up. Colin is dead? How?" She wiped her hands on a towel.

"Cancer. Luke said it was fast, and that Colin didn't want anyone to know. He didn't even tell his kids. He certainly never said anything to me when I spoke to him a few weeks ago. It's sad. He wasn't that old."

"That is sad," Shari agreed. "And his son now wants to sell this place?"

She nodded. "Luke told me that was his first thought, but he decided to come and see it first. We have to convince him to let us keep things running, that this could be a good investment for him. I just don't know how easy that will be. He's a complicated man."

Shari's gaze narrowed. "What aren't you telling me? How do you know so much about a guy who showed up a few hours ago?"

"Because he showed up in my life a long time ago. I told you that I had a personal connection to Colin; that's why he gave me the job when I was so clearly lacking in experience. Well, that personal connection was Luke. He was my college boyfriend. We dated for two years. We were madly in love, but we had a bad ending. Luke hasn't forgotten…or forgiven me."

"Did you cheat on him?"

"No, of course not. I wouldn't do that."

"Then what was so unforgiveable?"

"It's a long story."

"Give me the short version. I need to know what we're dealing with."

She let out a sigh. "Okay. Luke hated college. He thought he was just marking time on the way to his real life. After junior year, he decided to quit. He asked me to go with him for the summer. He was going to travel and start shooting film for the documentary series he eventually wanted to produce. At first, I said yes. It sounded romantic and fun to travel the world with him, but as the time grew closer to leaving, I panicked. I was so in love with him, I was afraid the summer wouldn't be enough, that I wouldn't come back, that I wouldn't finish school and have a chance to be the musician I wanted to be. So at the last second, I bailed. I didn't show up at the airport. I didn't tell him. I didn't answer his texts or his calls. I was a coward, and he was justifiably angry. Eventually, months later, we had a short communication, and I said it was over, and he said he knew that, and that was it. We haven't talked for ten years—until today."

Shari leaned against the counter. "Well, that's something. You didn't go with him to protect your future, and now he holds your future in his hands."

"I'm not unaware of the irony. Neither is he. There's a good chance he'll sell this place just to punish me."

"Is he that vengeful?"

She thought for a moment, thinking that the word really didn't describe Luke. "He didn't used to be. I don't know him anymore."

"You're going to need to get to know him again."

She took another sip of her coffee. "I don't know if he'll be here that long. I made a good pitch, Shari. I put all my personal feelings aside. I even showed him the tree that his parents carved their initials on. I tried to play on his sentimental side, on his love for his mom. And I told him that Kaitlyn needs this place and so do I. But I don't know if any of that will matter in the end. He's an adventurer, a wanderer. He travels light."

"What about money? Does he have the money to invest in this place? Does he need the cash? Is selling going to be his only alternative?"

"I don't know. He didn't say. Colin Brannigan was very wealthy. I assume some money is coming Luke's way. He didn't say that he had to sell it, only that he probably would."

"If he does have the money, then that gives us some hope. He could keep the resort going if he wants to."

"I think so. But Luke rarely does anything he doesn't want to do. And he's never wanted roots. I have a feeling this place looks like a huge weight to him."

"He doesn't have to live here."

"Exactly. That's the point we need to make—that this is a great place to visit, and we'll keep it running while he's traveling the world. He doesn't ever have to come here if he doesn't want to, but if he does want to, we have fun things for him to do. He loves nature and adventure. I think appealing to that side is probably the best bet."

"We'll help," Shari said. "Whatever Brad and I can do, and the rest of the staff will put in their best efforts, you know that. But you need to tell everyone what's at stake."

"I will at the staff meeting this afternoon. Brad mentioned that he's taking a group up to Wolmer Falls tomorrow. Maybe we can get him to stick around for that. He loves to hike. He'd probably want to go past Last Chance Rock because he is the ultimate daredevil."

A light suddenly entered Shari's eyes. "Wait a second. It's all making sense now. I thought I knew the name. Luke Brannigan—he makes the documentaries on extreme sports."

"Yes, that's him."

"I wondered if he was related to Colin. We have three of his DVDs. Brad loves Luke's films and his adventures. He's going to be over the moon when he hears Luke Brannigan might go hiking with him."

She smiled. "Good. Then he'll be inspired to get Luke to go."

"Definitely."

Shari tilted her head, her gaze thoughtful. "Tell me something, Liz. Do you still have feelings for Luke?"

"No, of course not. It's been a decade."

"That doesn't mean anything—not when you love someone."

"Well, I don't love him—not anymore."

Despite her words, her cheeks burned at the thought of their very recent passionate kiss. But that had just been a moment of insanity. They'd each wanted to know if the sparks were still there. And they were, but that didn't mean anything would happen. In the end, they'd be right back where they were before…Luke wanting to leave and her wanting to stay. She definitely didn't need a rerun of that painful show.

"It's okay, you know," Shari said, "if you still like him."

"It's definitely not okay," she replied. "I have too much to lose, and it's not just about me anymore. I have to consider Kaitlyn. She's been through so much, and she still has a long way to go. She's such a mixed-up, angry girl, and I can't blame her, but I can't seem to help her, at least not quickly. I need time. And that time has to be here."

"I know. I get it. Kaitlyn is a tough nut to crack. I thought we were getting along, but since I've gotten more visibly pregnant, she's pulled back. It's weird. Something about me being a mother bothers her."

"Maybe it makes her think about her own mom more. I don't know, either," Liz said. "But I hope one day I'll see her smile again, and not in that bored, sneering, sarcastic teenage way she occasionally does now—but the way she used to, when she was happy, when she was whole."

"It will happen; you just have to be patient. You're doing a good job with her, Liz. Someday she'll see how much you've given up for her."

"Not just for her, for my sister. Kelly saved me when we were little. She was more of a mom to me than my own mother. I owe her. I have to do right by Kaitlyn." She drew in a breath, then let it out. "But one problem at a time. Luke has now jumped to the top of my list, because if we have to leave here, I'm going to have to start all over again."

"I don't think that's the only reason he's at the top of your list," Shari said with a small laugh. "Tina said he's gorgeous."

"Yeah, well…I can't think about that."

"Good luck."

"Thanks. It's about time I had some good luck instead of bad."

Five

Luke hadn't thought he'd sleep, but somehow the shocks of the past few days combined with the jet lag had propelled him into oblivion. He rolled over onto his side, glancing at the clock on the bedside table. By the dark room, he knew the sun had set, but he was surprised to see it was almost eight o'clock. He'd been out for hours.

Getting out of bed, he walked over to the window, seeing the glow of a fire and hearing the faint sound of music. The campfire had obviously begun.

It didn't sound like his scene, but on the other hand, he was hungry, and Lizzie had said something about marshmallows. Maybe he could also beg for some kitchen leftovers. After all, he was the boss.

He shook his head at that still bewildering thought and knew he had some decisions to make, but not tonight, maybe not even tomorrow.

He liked speed. He liked to live a fast life, but this was too fast. He didn't want to get swept away on a current of emotion, and he felt more emotions than he liked swirling inside of him. He wasn't just coming off his father's unexpected death and the shocking knowledge that he'd never get to say good-bye, he was also having to deal with seeing Lizzie again.

Sitting down on the bed, he put on his shoes and then grabbed his phone as it rang. It was Knox.

"What's up?" he asked.

"I was going to ask you that question. How's the resort?"

"Not as big as it seemed when we were last here."

"I barely remember that trip."

"I didn't think I remembered it at all until I got here. That old guy still gives riding lessons. I thought he was a hundred back then, but he only appears to be about seventy now." He paused. "But the lodge didn't turn out to be the big surprise."

"I had a feeling there was more to it than just a random deed. Why did Dad leave you the resort?"

"Because Lizzie is here."

"Your Lizzie?" Knox asked in surprise.

"She hasn't been *my* Lizzie in a long time."

"I thought she was a pianist or something."

"Me, too, but her sister died, and she's now raising her niece. I guess Dad gave her the job managing the resort about six months ago."

"And he gave you the resort so you'd have to see her again. Interesting."

"So what did you get? Have you been to the storage unit yet?"

"Not yet. Too busy."

"Come on."

"I'll get there. Whatever it is, it isn't going anywhere."

"It could be Dad's Porsche or maybe his speedboat."

Knox laughed. "Yeah, like I'm going to be that lucky. How does Lizzie look?"

"Too good. I need to get out of here before I do something stupid." He'd actually already done something stupid, but he didn't need to share that with Knox.

"She's always been under your skin. You used to call her your beautiful trouble."

"That still fits. I thought I'd gotten her out from under my skin a long time ago. Her presence here complicates things, because she really needs the job, and as much as I know I don't owe her a damn thing, I feel for her situation."

"You could always keep the place."

"That's going to take some cash." His gaze drifted to the folder Lizzie had given him at lunch. He really needed to take a look at the accounting at some point. He didn't know if his dad had left him a profitable venture or a money pit.

"I'm sure there's probably some money set aside for it. Dad wouldn't leave you a burden."

"I don't know about that. He didn't like to make things easy for us. I need to go. Stay in touch."

"I will."

He got up from the bed, slipped his phone into his pocket and headed outside. He was halfway down the road when he heard raised voices along the river that ran behind the cabins. It sounded like kids— teenagers. He would have kept going, but there was something about the female voice that bothered him.

He walked around the back of the next cabin and saw two boys and a girl sitting on a fallen log that crossed the narrowest part of the river. It wasn't a particularly dangerous place to be. This part of the river was calm and not very deep. The rapids picked up a mile away when this stream connected with another.

The girl sat in the middle between the two teenage boys, and she was pushing away a bottle of vodka that one of the boys was trying to get her to drink.

He squinted through the shadows, realizing as he drew closer that the girl was Kaitlyn, and she didn't look very happy.

"Hey," he said loudly, striding down to the moonlit rocks. "What's going on?"

The boy grabbed the bottle and tossed it to the other side of the river. Then he and his friend ran across the log, jumped onto the opposite bank and disappeared into the trees.

Kaitlyn gave him an angry scowl as he drew closer, but he thought he saw a glint of relief in her eyes. Not that she'd admit it. He could see the rebellious fire building in her crossed arms and the stubborn set of her chin.

"Why did you do that?" she demanded.

"Do what? Ask a question? Who are your friends?"

"Nobody."

"Nobody with some alcohol."

"Everyone drinks; it's not a big deal."

"I used to say the same thing," he said, propping up his foot on the branch. "But I was a few years older than you when I got into vodka. And the first time I drank it, I got the meanest hangover. Consider yourself saved from that."

She didn't look like she cared about being saved.

"Are you going to tell my aunt?"

"I think you should do that."

"Maybe I will. Maybe then we can move away from this shit hole."

"I've lived in shit holes. This isn't one."

"Whatever. You have to say that, because you own the place."

"I'm saying it because it's true." He paused. "Look, I'm sorry about your parents. I knew them a long time ago. I liked them a lot."

"Why did you know them?" she asked suspiciously.

"Because I used to date your aunt."

"No way," she said, surprise flashing through her eyes. "You dated Aunt Liz? When?"

"When we were in college."

"I never heard that."

"I actually met you back then. You were an adorable three-year-old."

"I don't remember. Why did you break up?"

"We were young. We had some living to do."

"Are you going to get back together now?"

He didn't know why he hesitated. Of course they weren't getting back together. "No, I just came up to see the resort because my father died, and he left it to me."

"How did he die?"

"He got sick."

"So you got to say good-bye."

"Actually, I didn't." He picked up a pebble from the ground and spun it into the river. "I didn't get to say good-bye to either one of my parents."

"Your mom died, too?" she asked.

"When I was seven. She was also in a car crash. The kid who hit her had just gotten his license. It was a freak accident. She was in the hospital for a few days, but she never woke up, so we never said good-bye."

Kaitlyn's eyes widened. She looked like she wanted to say something, but she was forcing herself not to.

"Liz told me your parents died in a crash."

She jumped off the log, her feet landing in a few inches of water, but she didn't care; she was too intent on getting away from him.

"I'm sorry," he said quickly. "I shouldn't have said anything."

"It doesn't matter. They're dead. Talking about it isn't going to change that," she said with a defiant glint in her eyes.

"I know that's true. But..." He hesitated, not sure why he was going down this path with a girl he didn't even know. But there was something about her, something vulnerable, that bothered him. He didn't know how much trouble she would have gotten into with the boys and the alcohol if he hadn't come along, but he knew she was way too young for either one, and not just young but also fragile.

"But what?" she asked, giving him an angry glare that told him if he had something to say, he better say it fast.

"My dad would never talk about my mom after she died, and it made me feel like I couldn't talk about her. Sometimes I wanted to."

"Well, I don't want to. I've told everyone that. I just want to forget everyone and everything, because it's all gone." With that proclamation, she tossed her head and ran down the path toward the lodge.

He followed more slowly, wondering whether he should tell Liz what Kaitlyn had been up to. For her own safety, he knew he should, but he also knew that conversation would only drag him deeper into Liz's personal life.

Oh, hell, what did he have to lose? He'd already loved and lost her. He wasn't going back for round two, so he might as well try to help her deal with Kaitlyn.

The campfire was in full swing when he arrived. Kaitlyn squeezed in between two older women on the other side of the circle from Lizzie. She gave him a daring look, which made him smile. In some ways, she reminded him a little of his younger self. He was in no hurry to get her in trouble. In fact, he thought he'd let her sweat it out a bit.

His gaze moved to Lizzie. She was sitting next to a very pregnant woman. She gave him a wave and he walked over to join her. He was a little surprised at the welcome in her eyes, but he couldn't forget that he held her future in his hands, so it would be stupid to take any warm smile at face value.

"I'm glad you came," she said as he joined them. "This is Shari Jordan, our amazing chef—Luke Brannigan."

"Nice to meet you," he said, shaking Shari's hand. "And I definitely agree that your food is amazing. I had a great lunch earlier today."

"Thank you," Shari replied. "I wish my husband were here. He's a big fan of your films, but he had to run into town for something. Hopefully, you two will have a chance to meet up tomorrow."

"That would be great."

Shari got to her feet. "Why don't you take my place, Luke? I'm going to lie down. I don't think I need to hear Tom's story about Last Chance Rock again," she added with a laugh.

"Good-night," Lizzie said, then patted the empty bench next to her. "Have a seat, Luke. Tom is about to tell his favorite story."

"All right." His stomach was rumbling, but he decided he'd wait until the campfire dispersed before looking for food.

"I didn't think you were going to make it," Lizzie said.

"I fell asleep. The jet lag finally caught up to me."

"I'm surprised you even get jet lag as often as you travel."

"I am good at adjusting to new time zones, but the last few days were rougher than most."

"I'm sure."

"Who's Kaitlyn sitting with?" he asked.

"Nancy is the gray-haired woman. She's head of housekeeping. Karina is the blonde on the other side. She runs the arts and crafts program. They've both been here for over a decade. Your father kept on a lot of the staff when he bought the place."

"So that can happen," Luke remarked. "And it can turn out well."

Lizzie did not miss his point. "Sometimes it works out well. You never know what a new owner will want to do." She paused. "I think Tom is about to start."

He directed his gaze across the campfire.

"Once upon a time," Tom began, "it was rumored that there was gold at the top of the mountain behind us. It could be found only at the highest peak, nuggets as big as a man's fist. But it was impossible to get to. Many men tried. Many men died," Tom said in his deep, booming voice. "One day the son of a man who had perished in his attempt to get the gold decided he would climb to the top of the nearest peak and bring back the gold his father had spoken of. His mother said no, but in the early morning light this fourteen-year-old boy snuck out of his tent and went up the mountain."

Tom paused, and the crowd leaned forward in anticipation. "The young man climbed for hours. He was exhausted, his legs shaking, his will weakening, but he didn't want to let his father down. He wanted to bring the gold back to the family, to his mother and three younger sisters. He had just passed Wolmer Falls when the ground started to shake. He didn't know what was happening. The earth was moving. Rocks were falling. An enormous boulder, bigger than a one-story building, came flying down the mountain straight toward him. He jumped out of the way as the boulder crushed against the rocks, blocking the upper trail."

Tom took another breath, and Luke had to admit his own heart was pumping a little faster as he waited for the end of the story.

"The boy thought all was lost, but then he saw the sliver of light, the small opening where a person might squeeze past the boulder to get to the other side—to the mountain—to the gold. He stared at the boulder for a long minute. Was it a sign that his way was blocked? Should he turn back? But he knew there wouldn't be another time to try. They were leaving in the morning. Winter was coming. He had one last chance before the spring…"

Tom gave another dramatic pause, then continued. "The boy squeezed past the rock and climbed to the top of the mountain. The earth shook again as he reached the summit. And then he saw the most miraculous thing—gold. It was as bright and shiny as his father had described, even bigger than his fist. As he tried to pull it out of the dirt and the rocks that surrounded it, the earth began to shake again. The skies opened up and rain began to fall."

Tom lowered his voice another notch. "It was almost as if the mountain was weeping, as if the earth was begging the boy to leave the gold where it belonged. He looked into the sky and thought he saw the spirit of his father. He had done this for him—for the family, but his dad was waving at him to go back, to be safe, to live a long life and to leave the gold."

Tom looked around the campfire group. "The boy thought about what to do for a long minute and then he finally let go of the gold and got to his feet. Water came out of the sky, flying down the mountain, creating a massive waterfall where none had existed, and the gold he'd found was now behind a wall of water. The boy ran down the mountain as fast as he could, terrified the rushing water would catch up to him. He squeezed past the rock and made his way back here, the site of the camp. His mother was waiting and she hugged him as tight as she could, telling him she didn't want the gold; she wanted him to be safe. They left the next morning."

"To this day no one has ever found the gold behind the upper Wolmer Falls," Tom added. "Several men have made it all the way to the top, a few have died or been severely injured while trying, but no one has found the gold that the mountains refused to give up."

As Tom finished his story, a bunch of kids broke in with questions that Tom answered patiently.

"Was that supposed to be a cautionary tale?" Luke asked Lizzie.

She smiled. "I'm not sure. He tells a bunch of stories, and that's his favorite, but sometimes I worry he's only inspiring people to go after the gold." She tilted her head, giving him a speculative look. "I have a feeling you'd see only the challenge, not the caution."

"I have a feeling you'd be right. But I'm not motivated by gold."

"Just by the experience?"

"Exactly." His stomach rumbled. "You know, I missed dinner, and I have nothing in my cabin. Any chance you'd let me raid the kitchen?"

"Of course. We do have a snack kitchen for guests, but since you're the owner, I'll let you in the main kitchen. Shari made a vegetarian lasagna for dinner that's to die for."

"Lead the way," he said, getting to his feet.

"Sure. Let me just tell Kaitlyn where I'm going."

Liz had barely stood up when Kaitlyn came over and said she was going to bed.

"Do you want to get some food with us?" Liz asked. "We're going to the kitchen."

"Nope." Kaitlyn shot Luke a dark look, and then walked quickly toward the lodge.

"I guess she's not hungry," Liz said as they followed in Kaitlyn's steps. "I should probably just be happy that she even came to the campfire. I thought she might hang out with some of the kids who are here this week, but I didn't see them around."

As they entered the kitchen, he said, "Liz, I have to tell you something. I don't want to, but I think I should."

"What? You haven't already decided to sell the resort, have you? There's still so much to talk about."

He saw the panic in her eyes. "No, that's not what I want to talk to you about."

Relief ran through her eyes. "Oh, okay. What is it?"

"It's about Kaitlyn. When I left my cabin, I saw her at the river with two boys about her age. They were drinking something—vodka, I think. When I came along, they tossed the bottle into the woods and ran up the hill on the other side of the river."

Anger ran through her eyes. "Dammit. Those must have been the Harrison boys. She lied to me. She said she was hanging out with their sister, Julie, before the campfire."

"I didn't see another girl."

"So she went to the river with boys and booze? Were they just drinking, or…"

"Everyone was fully clothed, but it didn't look like the best situation. If it's any consolation, Kaitlyn said she hadn't been drinking, and it looked to me like she was saying no to taking the bottle when I got there."

"I guess I should be happy about that," she said, clearly discouraged. She leaned against the counter. "I don't know what I'm doing, Luke. I don't know how to be a mother, especially not to an angry, sad, thirteen-year-old, who is determined to ruin her life as fast as she can. Maybe I should have stayed in LA, or at least closer to therapy, but she hated going there, and even the doctor said they weren't getting very far, that

Kaitlyn was stubbornly determined to keep her thoughts private. I thought she might open up to me if I could get her alone, away from all the memories, but that hasn't happened. I seem to be the last person she wants to talk to. She used to like me. Now she hates me. I don't know what happened."

"Her parents died; that's what happened."

"I want to help her through her grief, but I don't know how."

"Maybe she just needs to get through it herself."

"I tell myself that, but then I wonder as time passes, is she getting more screwed up?"

He gave her a sympathetic smile. "I'm sure you're doing your best."

"Which might not be good enough." She pushed away from the counter. "I should get you that lasagna."

She opened the refrigerator door and started pulling out plastic containers. "We also have salad and fruit to go with it."

"I'll take it all."

She smiled. "You always had a big appetite."

"I did," he admitted, thinking that she'd been his biggest hunger.

She must have seen something in his eyes, because she immediately shook her head and gave him a warning look. "None of that, Luke."

"None of what?"

"You know. We need to keep things professional from here on out."

"If I was keeping everything strictly professional, I'd already be on the phone to my brother Gabe asking him to list the property for sale."

"Really? I'm the only reason you're not doing

that?" she asked, setting the food containers on the island.

"I do have a heart. I know things are rough for you and Kaitlyn. That gives me something to think about, so let's not lie to each other and say this is just business."

"Okay. I appreciate you taking us into consideration. I do think I can prove to you that the resort is a good investment, too."

"Because I'm so interested in investment," he said dryly.

"It's an interesting way to make money, and you always liked interesting," she reminded him.

He smiled. "You know me too well."

"I used to."

"I haven't changed that much, and you can work on me tomorrow," he said, scooping some lasagna onto a plate, then putting it in the microwave. "Right now I'm more interested in food."

"I can live with that."

Fifteen minutes later, he sat on a stool at the kitchen island, finishing off a big plate of pasta while Liz sat across from him, sipping coffee and stabbing at random blueberries in the bowl of fruit between them.

"You could get yourself a plate," he said, reminded of all the times Liz had told him she wasn't hungry, then proceeded to eat half of his food.

She gave him a guilty smile. "Sorry. I like blueberries."

"So do I," he said pointedly.

She set down her fork. "I'm done; it's all yours."

"I was kidding. We can share."

"It's fine."

As she sipped her coffee, he said, "Tell me about your life before your sister died. What were you doing? Where were you living?"

"I was in New York, sharing a teeny, tiny apartment with a violinist named Gretchen Goldsmith. We both played for the New York Philharmonic."

"That sounds impressive."

"It was just one of several dreams that came true. I played at Carnegie Hall, Luke. I was so nervous, I was shaking; I wasn't sure I could play, but somehow I did."

He smiled at the look of triumph and pride in her eyes. "I wish I could have seen that." As he said the words, he realized he meant them. He'd been so angry with her for so many years that he hadn't allowed himself to even think about what she was doing. But he'd been there when she was a struggling student with a big dream. Now he regretted that he hadn't seen her reach that dream.

"It was amazing," she said. "But it wasn't just the big events that were exciting. I played for the Royal Ballet at one performance. I even played for a rock musician at a recording session. He wanted a classical background piano."

"Who was that?"

"Beck Robbins."

"He's huge."

She shrugged. "His ego is huge, too. It was fun, but he wasn't the nicest guy to work for."

"It sounds like you've done well, Lizzie."

"I have. New York was exciting, energetic, and super-fast—maybe a little too fast at times. It took me awhile to find my feet, hail cabs with the determination of a native New Yorker, push my way to the front of the hot dog line, fight for a seat on the subway. But eventually I adapted. I wasn't making a fortune, but I was doing what I loved."

"That's what it's all about. I'm happy for you. I mean that."

"Thanks," she said, her gaze connecting with his. "I'm happy that you've lived the life you dreamed about, too. You've probably been around the world twice."

"There are still places I haven't been yet. I like to get away from the big cities, see where the locals really live."

"And where you can see the stars," she said as they exchanged another remembered smile.

"I do like the stars," he admitted.

"I used to think that if you didn't do what you've been doing, that you would have been a good astronomer."

"Too much school for me."

"But you already know the names of all the stars."

"Not all of them," he said with a laugh. "But I have to say that I've seen amazing light shows from some of the highest mountain peaks in the world."

"And here I was just about to tell you that there's a rooftop patio perfect for stargazing."

"Good to know."

She licked her lips, and her eyes darkened, and he wanted nothing more than to lean across the island and kiss her again.

She must have read his mind, because she was suddenly on her feet. "I should talk to Kaitlyn," she said.

He was disappointed, but maybe it was for the best. He rose. "I'll clean up."

"No, I'll come back and do that later."

"I don't think cleaning up after me is in your job description."

"It's a few plates, and I know where everything goes. Really, it's fine. I'll walk you out so I can lock up."

She moved to the door, waiting for him to follow.

"Thanks for the meal," he said, as they left the kitchen.

"Of course."

As they walked through the dining room into the living room, he paused at the sight of the piano in the corner. "I remember that piano—or at least one that looked like that one. My mom used to sing at night with some of the other guests." He shook his head. "So strange, the memories that come back to me of her."

"You never talked about your mom when we were together."

"Not much to talk about. I barely remember her. Just bits and pieces come into my head, usually only when I'm around family or the house where I grew up, but being here reminds me of those family trips we used to take together."

"It's nice to have some memories. I don't remember my father at all. He didn't die, but he was gone before my third birthday."

"Do you know where he is? Have you ever seen him?"

"No to both questions. I have no interest in looking for him. He abandoned us. There's really nothing more to know."

"How's your mother?"

"She's the same. She still works at the salon, at

least a couple of days a week. She has her battles with depression and alcohol. She can be good for a while, and then she's not. She fell apart after Kelly died. Kelly didn't just take care of me when we were growing up; she took care of my mom, too. But I think she's pulling herself out of the deep sadness. She called the other day to ask how Kaitlyn was; I thought that was a good sign."

He thought it was impressive that Lizzie had always been able to cut her mother slack for not being that great of a mom. But Lizzie had a big heart and the ability to understand that everyone had a weakness, everyone had a flaw. She used to tell him that she really believed the other side of a weakness was a strength, and you just have to find it.

Funny, he hadn't remembered that until now, but it was something that had helped him persevere when he thought he was too tired or too frustrated or too impatient to get to where he needed to go. Certainly impatience to have it all was one of his flaws. On the other hand, it was that impatience that drove him.

Lizzie had never been impatient. She'd been driven to succeed in music, but she'd been willing to play the scales over and over again, go to class, take tests, prepare and prepare and prepare. That dedication probably wasn't her flaw, but it had sometimes annoyed him when he'd wanted her to jump or take a risk and she'd wanted to assess every potential outcome, which usually meant he went ahead without her.

"What are you thinking about?" she asked curiously. "You have an odd look on your face."

"Just remembering how we used to be together."

"You really shouldn't keep going back there,

Luke. We're not those people anymore. We've both changed. We've grown up."

He smiled. "You probably more than me."

She smiled back at him. "You said it; I didn't."

"Why don't you play something for me?"

"No," she said quickly, giving a vehement shake of her head. "I don't play that piano."

"Why? Is it out of tune?"

"No, but I just don't play it." Shadows filled her eyes. "I can't, Luke."

"Why? Are you afraid you'll want your old life back?"

"Maybe."

"Music can still be in your life even if you're not playing in an orchestra."

"I don't think it can."

"But you love to play. When I used to watch you…I sometimes felt a little jealous."

Surprise passed through her eyes. "Why?"

"Because the music transported you. It took you away from me—to a place I couldn't go. You'd get this look on your face, and you were gone. I didn't like that."

"I was probably thinking about you, Luke. That happened a lot back then—even when I was playing. For a while there, you were in every breath I took." She paused. "Love is different when you're young, when you have everything in front of you."

"You're not exactly old now, Lizzie. You don't turn thirty for another month."

"Some days I feel like I'm a hundred. Anyway…" She moved toward the staircase in the lobby. "I'll see you tomorrow."

As she went upstairs, he found himself watching

her until she disappeared from view, remembering her words—*you were in every breath I took.*

She'd been in every breath he'd taken, too. He hadn't really thought of it that way, but it was true.

On the other hand, if their love had been that strong, why hadn't either of them fought for it? Maybe it was only now that they could see what they'd had. But it didn't matter.

It was too late to go back. Wasn't it?

Six

Liz forced herself not to look back at Luke as she went up the stairs and entered the two-bedroom apartment on the top floor that she shared with Kaitlyn. Their bedrooms were separated by a living room and kitchenette, which they rarely occupied at the same time. In fact, Kaitlyn was usually in her room with the door closed, her headphones on, and either her phone or computer holding all of her attention.

She should probably force Kaitlyn to use the computer in a more public space, but she had so many battles to fight on so many fronts that she just hadn't gotten to that one yet. She knocked on Kaitlyn's door and then pushed it open when she didn't get an answer. Kaitlyn rarely answered since she usually couldn't hear the knock, or at least she pretended not to.

She walked into the room, seeing her niece sitting back against the pillows on her bed, looking at something on her computer with her headphones on, as she'd predicted.

"I want to talk to you," she said loudly, taking a seat on the bed.

"What?" Kaitlyn asked aggressively, pulling her headphones off. She gave Liz a burning glare, as if she'd decided that offense was the best defense.

"You lied to me, Kaitlyn. You went to the river with two boys and a bottle of alcohol."

"I knew he'd tell you."

"Of course Luke told me. What you did was reckless and possibly dangerous."

"It was no big deal. They're just kids."

"What happened?"

"Nothing. We were talking."

"And drinking."

"I wasn't drinking."

"But they were."

Kaitlyn shrugged. "Everyone drinks. It's not a big deal."

"At thirteen? I don't think that's true."

"You never believe me, so why should now be different?"

Lizzie frowned at the accusation. "What do you mean I never believe you? What are you talking about?"

"Nothing."

"Dammit, Kaitlyn. You have to talk to me."

"We are talking. You just don't like what you're hearing," Kaitlyn retorted.

She let out a sigh. "I want you to be safe, honey. You've been through the worst kind of pain, and I know you're still hurting. I want to help." There was no response from her niece. Liz stared at the hard wall of defiance in Kaitlyn's eyes and didn't even see one tiny crack she could wiggle through, but she still had to try. "It's up to me to protect you now. That's what your mom would want. But I need your help; I can't do it alone."

Kaitlyn shook her head, her lips tightening with scorn. "You have no idea what my mom would want. You saw us like three times in the last six years. Mom used to cry because you wouldn't come visit for Christmas. She said you were too busy for us."

"That's..." She floundered, searching for the right words. It was true that she'd missed the last few Christmas holidays, but she'd kept in touch with Kelly. "We talked on the phone, Kaitlyn. Your mom and I kept in touch even when we weren't together."

"Yeah, and then she'd hang up the phone and cry. She said you loved music more than us."

She was stunned and hurt by Kaitlyn's words. Were they true? Had Kelly cried because they didn't see each other that often? Had she put her own needs ahead of her sister? Had she loved music more than her family?

"Are we done now?" Kaitlyn demanded.

Since she was still somewhat speechless, she got up from the bed and walked to the door. Then she paused. Was her niece playing her? Had she drummed up a story to turn the conversation away from her bad behavior?

Unfortunately, there was no way to be sure.

Drawing in a deep breath, she walked back to the bed.

Kaitlyn gave her another long-suffering sigh.

"You lied to me, Kaitlyn," she said. "To make up for that, you're going to help Tom clean out the stables in the morning. Seven a.m.; don't be late."

Kaitlyn stared back at her, but she didn't say anything.

Lizzie walked out of the room, shutting the door behind her. She let out a breath, wondering if she was doing the right thing or the wrong thing. Being a mother was a lot more complicated and far more difficult than she'd ever imagined, especially when the kid she was trying to mother hated her guts.

—⇒⇒⇐⇐—

Luke walked into the stables early Thursday morning. Tom gave him a friendly smile as he finished feeding carrots to a beautiful brown horse.

"Morning," Tom said. "Rumor has it you're the new boss."

"Luke Brannigan," he said, extending his hand.

"Tom Gordon. I remember you. Daredevil boy. Wanted to jump over a fence at the end of your first riding lesson."

Tom's words took him a long way back. "How could you possibly remember that?" he asked.

"Faces stick in my head—names not so much. Plus, there was a bunch of you boys running around. You used to come twice a year until your mom died. She was a sweetheart. Your dad was head over heels for her. Never thought he liked the place that much, but she did. Was shocked as could be when he bought it two years ago."

"I was surprised about that, too. I didn't actually learn about it until a few days ago."

"I'm sorry about his passing."

"Thanks," he said shortly.

"What can I do for you today?" Tom asked.

"I was thinking about taking a ride, but I haven't been on a horse in about twenty years."

"It's just like riding a bike."

He smiled. "I certainly hope so."

"We've got a couple of nice, easy-going mares, but somehow I don't think they'll be to your taste, not if you're the way you used to be."

"If you mean reckless and addicted to speed, then you'd be right," Lizzie interrupted with a smile.

"I have never been reckless on a horse," he said, a little unsettled by how happy he was to see her. Even in faded jeans and a T-shirt, little makeup on, and her blonde hair in a ponytail, she was breathtakingly pretty.

"That might be the only place you've been cautious," she retorted. She looked at Tom. "Maybe Daisy?"

Tom nodded. "I was thinking the same. I'll saddle her up. You'll want Vixen, of course."

"Hang on, I get a horse named Daisy and Liz gets one named Vixen? That doesn't seem right," he said.

Liz smiled. "I'm not riding with you, and if you want Vixen, you can have her, but sometimes she gets stubborn and just decides to take a break until you sweet-talk her into moving again. That's why she's called Vixen."

"The last thing I want to do this morning is sweet-talk a horse, so I'll take Daisy, but you are coming with me."

"I have work to do."

"It's seven."

"And breakfast is starting."

"You don't run the kitchen, do you?" he challenged.

"I help out," she said defensively. "I came down here to check on Kaitlyn. She's supposed to be helping Tom clean out the stalls as punishment for lying to me last night." She looked around the barn. "I don't see her, but she's not in her room."

"She's out back," Tom said. "She's brushing down Chestnut."

"Hopefully with not too much attitude," Lizzie said.

"She's different with the horses," Tom replied. "They speak her language."

"I wish I did," Lizzie muttered. "But I guess I'll leave her alone."

"Great, then you're coming with me," Luke said. "You want me to see everything the resort has to offer, so let's take a ride."

She hesitated, obviously torn between wanting to keep her distance and wanting to get him on her side.

"I'll get Daisy and Vixen ready," Tom said with a knowing smile. "You two can figure out the rest."

"I think you sold Vixen short," Luke told Liz as they made their way down a shady trail a half hour later. "She seems more than happy to lead the way whereas Daisy seems half asleep. Can we go any slower?"

Liz flung him a smile. "Don't worry. Daisy can run. She just needs a little space, a wider trail; she doesn't like to force anything."

"You know a lot about your horses."

"I've spent some time riding. The horses are the only thing Kaitlyn likes about the resort, so I've actually gotten her to go riding a few times."

"So mucking out stalls might not have been much of a punishment," he said.

"Well, she hates getting up early, so I thought that might be worth something."

"I don't remember you getting up this early back in the day." He thought about all the lazy mornings they'd spent in bed together, usually because Lizzie just hadn't been ready to get up yet. Sometimes he'd hold a cup of coffee hostage just so he could fool around with her a bit more. He smiled at the memory.

"My sleepy mornings were one of the things you didn't like about me," she said lightly.

"I'm sure I never said I wanted you out of my bed."

"You know what I mean. You were usually impatient to get on with the day. When we weren't going to class, you had something planned: a hike, a run, a surfing lesson, bike riding down the coast…you never sat still."

"That's called living, Lizzie."

"You can relax and enjoy life, too. You don't have to take everything at a dead sprint."

"Only way I know how to do it." He paused. "Are you still a caffeine addict?"

"Guilty. I love coffee. I can't deny it. My brain doesn't work until I have my first cup."

"How many cups have you had today?"

"Only one. I try to pace myself." She glanced at him, then waved her hand at the trees surrounding them. "It is beautiful here, don't you think?"

He nodded. "You don't have to sell me on one of the most beautiful valleys in the world."

"What do I need to sell you on?"

Her question made him think for a moment. "I don't really know."

"Your dad must have had a reason for leaving you this particular piece of property. What do you think that was?"

He gave her a smile. "I think the reason was you."

"Don't be ridiculous," she said, shaking her head. "I wouldn't have been a factor. I'm sure it had more to do with your love of the outdoors than anything else. He probably thought you would love it here."

"That might have been his second thought; his first thought was you, throwing us back together."

"Why?"

"Because he liked you. He thought you were good for me. You had your feet on the ground. You weren't going to do something stupid."

She frowned. "That makes me sound like a really boring and very heavy anchor."

"Well, if it makes you feel better, I didn't see you that way."

"Good. I know I'm not as daring as you, but I did sneak into the cafeteria after hours with you. Let's not forget that. And what about that time I prank-called your brother James and pretended to be a collection agency?"

He laughed at the memory. James had been acting so cocky about his early business decisions that he'd decided to throw him a curve ball. "I forgot about that. You were very convincing. And James never knew it was me, either."

"So I wasn't that boring, right?"

He sensed there was more behind the question than she wanted to admit. He met her gaze and said, "You were never boring, Lizzie."

"I sense there's a *but* coming after that statement."

"But," he said. "My dad was right. You were more grounded than me, more practical, more focused on the details and I was all big picture."

"Maybe that's because we grew up so differently. I didn't have the kind of money you had. There was no one around who would or could bail me out if I got into trouble."

"I never asked anyone to bail me out, either," he returned quickly.

"I know you didn't, because you're proud and you don't like to ask for help, but still you didn't have to worry about your tuition for the next semester, or your rent money. You didn't have to make bean and cheese burritos every day and go home with the smell clinging to your hands and your clothes."

"Those burritos were good."

"Yours were good, because I made them extra special," she said, smiling back at him. "Sometimes I even snuck in some chicken."

"I appreciated that. And you're right, you did have to work harder than me back then. I took some of the basics in life for granted." He paused. "My dad wasn't wrong about you, Lizzie. You were good for me. You pushed me to try new things. Remember the ballroom dancing class? And all those concerts you took me to so I could listen to Bach, and Beethoven, and Mozart? I even took that music appreciation class with you."

She smiled. "I forgot about that. You used to complain, but I think you secretly liked it."

"I liked you." He drew in a breath. "We were good together." He realized now that the blinding anger over the way things had ended had prevented him from remembering the happier times.

"For a while anyway," she agreed. "We balanced each other out. But we ended up going in different directions."

"Until now," he said with a smile as Vixen came to an abrupt stop to inspect some low-hanging branches.

"Damn," she said. "We were doing so well. I thought Vixen would behave."

"And here I thought you were more worried that I'd behave." He pulled Daisy up next to Vixen. "So what do we do?"

"She'll move along in a minute."

"Sure about that?" he teased. "Maybe you should try some sweet talk. You could always get me revved up."

She shot him a dark look. "You were always revved up."

He laughed. "That's probably true. A smile from you was all it took."

She shook her head and patted Vixen. "Come on, baby, let's keep walking. More trees ahead."

Finally, Vixen lifted her head and began to move slowly down the path. Lizzie glanced over at him. "Tell me what you're working on now, Luke. Do you have a new film coming out?"

"In a few months, yes. We just finished the last shot. I did a base jump off a mountain in Norway."

"Of course you did," she said dryly.

"I think we got some great footage. My partner Pete was operating a camera via drone, which now allows us to capture new, exciting angles."

"So you don't have to actually jump anymore?"

"Well, I don't have to…"

"But you want to."

"It's part of the honest and true experience. I narrate how I'm feeling, what the conditions are, who's there with me, what I know about the area."

"Base jumping is when you jump off a cliff and open up a chute before you die?"

"That sums it up," he said with a grin.

She shook her head. "And you're never scared?"

"I wouldn't say that. Fear is part of it, of course. I just don't let it stop me."

"Is the film just about base jumping?"

"No, the broader subject is the way people fly: base jumping, parachuting, helicopter skiing, anything that takes them through the air."

"There are a lot of crazy people in the world."

"I prefer to call them adventurous."

"You would," she said. "I have to admit that I was always in awe of your courage. You inspired me to step out of my comfort zone. I know, in your opinion, I probably didn't go too far, but farther than I would have gone on my own."

He was surprised she'd admit that.

She glanced over at him. "When I didn't show up at the airport, I thought to myself: if you're going to break up with this incredible guy in order to make your career happen, then you better make it happen. I had to prove to myself that I hadn't made the wrong choice. So I fought really hard and went on a lot of painful auditions to get to the places I told you about earlier. Maybe I wouldn't have been so strong in that pursuit if I didn't have you in the back of my head."

"I—I don't know what to say to that," he murmured. "You're welcome?"

"You should have stopped with I don't know what to say to that."

He smiled. "I'm glad I inspired you in some way. I really am happy for your success. I wouldn't have been ten years ago or even five years ago, but now that I've hit thirty—"

"And you're older and wiser," she interrupted.

"Exactly. I see things more clearly." He shook his head. "It's strange how we never talked after the day you finally returned my call."

"I talked to you in my head a hundred times. I thought about picking up the phone, sending a text, but then I just couldn't. I couldn't open that door again. There didn't seem to be a point."

He'd felt much the same way. "Well, my father opened the door and shoved us both through it."

"Yes, he did," she muttered.

For the next few moments, they rode in silence. As the trail widened, Lizzie nudged Vixen into a faster trot and Daisy followed. "Now, this is more like riding," he said, as they picked up speed.

"This is a good spot to run," she said, as her hair flew out behind her, and her smile radiated the same happiness he felt to be flying over the ground.

It wasn't like jumping off a cliff, but it was fun.

Their gallop came to a halt about ten minutes later when they had to move single file along the river. Eventually, Vixen called another halt in the shade of some very tall trees.

"I guess we're stopping," Lizzie said with a shrug.

"That was a nice ride."

"I'm glad you liked it."

"So, what happened with Kaitlyn? I know you said you punished her for lying; did she tell you what happened?"

"Not really. She actually turned the tables on me.

I made the mistake of saying that I wanted to protect her the way her mother would have wanted me to do, and suddenly she was all over me about how I didn't know what her mother would want. She came out swinging hard, bringing up stuff I didn't know about and am not even sure is true."

"Like what?" he asked curiously.

"She said Kelly was angry and sad that I didn't go to visit her the last few Christmas holidays, that Kelly would cry when she got off the phone with me. She said Kelly thought I was selfish after all she'd done for me. Kaitlyn made me feel really guilty and really bad. Because I never meant to hurt my sister. I loved her. But Kaitlyn said that Kelly told her I loved music more. Maybe it's no wonder Kaitlyn doesn't want to live with me. It might have nothing to do with the tragic death of her parents and more to do with the fact that she doesn't like me, that she blames me for making her mother sad."

He saw the emotions run through Lizzie's eyes. "I don't know what you did or didn't do, but I know this: you loved your sister, and she loved you, no matter what distance was between you."

"I thought so," she said, looking like she really wanted to believe him. "We did drift apart a little, but we led different lives. Kelly was a wife and a mom, and she was entrenched in her world of suburbia, carpools, and PTA meetings. I didn't think it bothered her that I didn't come home for Christmas. She had her husband's family there, and Mom usually showed up." She sighed. "I'm rationalizing, aren't I?"

"It sounds like normal sibling stuff to me. I don't see my brothers all that much. We're all living our lives. I think Kaitlyn just wanted to make you feel bad, take the focus off herself."

"That's certainly possible."

"So don't let her get to you, don't let her doubt your relationship with your sister."

"I'm going to try not to. I just wish I could put a small dent in the wall Kaitlyn has put up around her."

"That will probably just take time. The more you're together—"

"That's the thing; we don't do much together. I've gotten her to go riding with me twice, but she doesn't talk to me. She'll sit in a lounger at the pool when I'm out there, but again, she doesn't talk to me. She's listening to her music or texting her friends at home. I can't get her to go on a hike or a river trip. She says no to every single invitation that involves leaving the immediate area, so I don't know how I'm ever going to get through to her."

"Well, I'm not a psychologist, but…"

"But you feel qualified to give me some advice? Why am I not surprised? You love to give advice."

"And you usually don't take it."

"Neither do you," she retorted. "Fine. What's your diagnosis, Doc?"

"Kaitlyn lost her whole life, her parents, her home, her school, and her friends. Maybe to survive, she has to find some part of her life she can control, like not listening to you, not doing the things you want her to do."

Lizzie nodded. "I get it. Saying no is her way of being in charge of something. That thought has occurred to me as well."

"Damn, I thought I'd come up with something brilliant," he said lightly.

She laughed. "You've never thought less than

highly of yourself. The Brannigan brothers have never been short on confidence. Speaking of which, what are your brothers doing these days?"

"Knox works at a bar called The Wake in Santa Monica."

"Sounds about right. What about everyone else? Is James on his way to making his first million?"

"No, he's well past his first million. He runs a very successful hedge fund."

"I've never understood what those are."

"Let's just say he moves and makes a lot of money for a lot of people. He takes after my dad. So does Gabe. He runs a highly successful real-estate company. His last grateful client gave him an Aston Martin as a thank-you."

"Wow. He must have done some job."

"I guess. Max is out of the service but cagey about what he's doing now. Finn is flying for the Navy. I haven't seen either one of them in a few years. Hunter is a photojournalist. He travels to hot spots in the world. Our paths have crossed a few times, sometimes in the strangest places."

"And all still single? No one has managed to snag one of the handsome Brannigan brothers?"

"Not yet."

"I wonder who will be the first."

"No idea." Although, as he looked at Lizzie, he couldn't help wondering if he might have gotten married first if he'd stayed with her. But that was a crazy thought.

"We should go back," Lizzie said, turning Vixen back around. "I need to get to work. I don't want the boss to think I'm a slacker."

"I could never think that."

She tossed her head, gave him a smile and Vixen a kick, and soon they were headed back to the barn. He was sorry the ride was coming to an end. The conversation between him and Lizzie had been a long time coming, and he wasn't quite ready to say it was over yet.

Seven

—⟫⟪—

They arrived back to the stables a little after eight, and Lizzie felt happier and more carefree than she had in months. It had also been awhile since she'd been able to remember the time she'd spent with Luke in a non-regretful way. Because, of course, she'd had regrets. She'd worried for years after the breakup that she'd made the wrong choice. But by then, it was too late to go back.

And it was too late to go back now, she told herself forcefully, as she got off Vixen and handed her horse to one of the stable hands. Whether or not Luke kept the resort as an investment, he wouldn't be staying here, and she would be. Another good-bye was just around the corner.

"I'm ready for breakfast," Luke said, falling into step with her as they walked toward the lodge.

"Me, too. I highly recommend the blueberry pancakes, the French toast, or Shari's omelet of the day. She uses whatever fresh vegetables are in season, and it's always delicious."

"What if I have all three?"

"You could do that."

"Shari looks very pregnant. Who's going to cook when she's having her baby?"

"Still to be determined," she replied, as they entered the lodge. "She's been a little slow on interviewing replacement chefs. She's very territorial when it comes to her kitchen. But I think she has someone coming tomorrow or sometime this weekend. Once we get past Labor Day weekend, things slow down, so it will be an easier time to bring someone in."

"How slow does it get?"

"Not completely dead. The fall is beautiful and often warm, and sometimes we get the more serious rock climbers and hikers in September and October." As they walked into the dining room, she added, "I want to introduce you to Brad Jordan, Shari's husband, and also the head of our adventure programs. He's right over here."

She led the way to a nearby table where Brad was finishing up his breakfast. Brad was thirty-six years old with sandy-brown hair, green eyes, and a boyish smile. He had an outgoing, energetic personality, and she'd never met a guest yet who hadn't enjoyed one of his guided hiking trips.

"Brad, I want you to meet Luke Brannigan."

Brad got to his feet, excitement in his eyes when he shook hands with Luke, and she had a feeling a bromance was quite possibly in the works between these two, and why not—they were cut from the same cloth, although Brad's adventures didn't come close to what Luke had accomplished.

"I can't believe you're the new owner," Brad said.

"I didn't even realize you were related to Colin Brannigan. He's never been out here, so he was just a name on the letterhead. But I know you, or at least your work. I have all three of your films on DVD. I've watched them each a half-dozen times."

"Thanks," Luke said. "I'm glad you liked them."

"Like them? They're amazing. You capture moments that are literally magic…and sometimes terrifying. *Do you ever think what the hell am I doing?*"

"I can answer that," Lizzie cut in. "Luke never asks that question."

Luke gave her a smile. "That was the old me. Believe it or not, I have asked myself that a few times in recent years as the challenges have become more complex."

"Really?" she asked doubtfully. "Then you have changed."

"I got older and smarter."

"But it doesn't stop you from going for broke."

"No, it doesn't," he said. "What's life without some risk?"

"I'd love to take you up to Wolmer Falls," Brad said, drawing the conversation back to him. "I've got a group leaving at eleven. Why don't you join us? It's an easy hike and certainly won't be an extreme adventure like you're used to, but the falls are good this time of year, and I think you'd enjoy it."

"You should go," she encouraged. "I know you like to be active."

"Are you going?" he asked.

"No, I leave the hiking to Brad and his staff. I have work to do here."

"Can someone cover for you?"

"Well, maybe, but you don't need me. Brad can show you everything."

"You should come," Brad said. "You haven't gone on a hike since you've been here. Neither has Kaitlyn. Why don't you both join us? The Harrisons and their three teenagers are coming. I think Kaitlyn would have fun."

"You've never been on a hike?" Luke challenged.

"I've been busy, and I'm not on vacation."

"Still, you'd be able to give a better testimonial if you experienced the actual hike. Brad says it's easy."

"It is," Brad reassured her.

She looked into both men's faces and saw matching smiles of determination. Brad probably sensed he wasn't getting Luke without her. And Luke was making it clear that if she wanted him to stick around, she was going to have to spend more time with him.

"I guess I could go," she said slowly. "Tina is working today, and most of our arrivals won't be coming in until four."

"Perfect," Luke said.

She thought it was anything but perfect. The horseback ride had been fun. She'd enjoyed it more than she wanted to admit. But that was part of the problem. Spending more time with Luke was not going to make their inevitable good-bye easier to stomach.

Her gaze moved to the door as Kaitlyn entered the dining room with her headphones on. Even though she didn't trust the Harrison boys, their parents were going on the hike, and it would be nice to get Kaitlyn away from the property. She waved her niece over. Kaitlyn gave her the usual irritated look, but walked over to them.

"We're going on a hike to Wolmer Falls," she told her. "Brad, Luke, and the Harrisons and their kids. I'm going to go as well. Why don't you come along?"

Kaitlyn immediately shook her head. "No way."

"It will be fun. It's an easy hike."

"I don't want to go, and you can't make me," Kaitlyn proclaimed. With that, she turned away and ran out of the room.

"I guess Kaitlyn's not going," she muttered. "I thought the other kids might have been an enticement for her, but I guess not."

"She'll do it when she's ready," Luke said, sympathy in his eyes.

She shrugged. "We'll see."

"I'll meet you both out front at eleven," Brad told them. "Have a good breakfast. Fuel up for the hike."

"We will." As she sat down across from the most attractive man she'd ever been with, she had a feeling she was going to need more than fuel to get her through the rest of the day. And what about tomorrow and the next day? She wanted Luke to keep the resort so she could hold on to her job, but how was she going to handle him being her boss and nothing more?

Not that she wanted something more…oh, who was she kidding…of course, she wanted more. She hadn't stopped thinking about his kiss all night. But that was the problem. He'd always been dangerous to her life plans, her goals. He could derail her life with so little effort.

Luke gave her an odd look as their eyes met. "What?" he asked.

She shook her head. "I have no words."

For some reason, he seemed to understand her

cryptic statement.

"Some days you don't need words, at least not important words," he said. "Let's make that day today."

"Deal."

True to their bargain, they discussed nothing of importance over omelets, hash browns, and turkey bacon. She introduced Luke to some of the staff members who wandered into the dining room, noting how friendly and welcoming he was with each and every one of them. Luke had always had the ability to fit in anywhere. He was genuinely interested in getting to know people, and they responded to him in kind.

When he got into a lengthy conversation with John, one of Brad's rock-climbing guides, she excused herself and went into the kitchen to speak to Shari.

"I hear you're finally going hiking," Shari said as she took a sheet of cookies out of the oven. "And that Luke was the deciding vote."

"Trying to keep the boss happy," she replied. "I was hoping Kaitlyn would go, but she said no."

"Yes. Brad said she shot down the idea very quickly."

"I hate to leave her here on her own."

"She'll be fine. It's a warm day. I'm sure she'll be out at the pool."

The pool was one of Kaitlyn's favorite spots. "True, and I'll have the wild boys on the hike with me, so I don't have to worry about them." She paused, seeing Shari rub her abdomen. "Everything okay?"

"Just a little twinge. I'm getting so big, and I still have another month to go."

"Which reminds me—we really need to hire

another chef soon." She looked around the kitchen to make sure their part-time sous chef was not in the room. "I don't think Michelle is skilled enough to take over for you. She's a sweet girl, and she's learning quickly, but she can't run the kitchen."

"I know," Shari said wearily, brushing a strand of hair out of her eyes. "I thought I could train Michelle to be better faster, but while she's great at soups and stews and casseroles, she's a disaster with anything baked and she seems unable to grill meat with any kind of finesse. Plus, her time management skills are not the best."

"Let's get the ad up tomorrow wherever it needs to go."

Shari nodded. "I've got it written on my computer; I'll email it to you this afternoon. I want to take another look at it."

"Great."

"By the way, Brad is so excited about hanging out with Luke."

She smiled. "I saw the love in his eyes."

"Is that because you know what love for Luke looks like?" Shari teased.

"We were over a long time ago. I told you that."

"Sometimes love is better the second time around."

"Or sometimes it ends the exact same way—with a broken heart. No thanks. I have enough problems." She headed toward the door. "I'll check in with you when I get back."

"Have fun. I'm going to pack up some cookies for the hike."

"Now that makes me more excited about walking two miles up a hill."

After leaving the kitchen, she caught up with some paperwork, checked in with her staff on arriving and departing guests and then made her way upstairs a little before eleven to change her clothes.

On her way back downstairs, she checked on Kaitlyn, who was on her bed watching something on her computer.

"Hey," she said. "It's a nice day. Don't you want to be outside?"

Kaitlyn shrugged.

"Tom said you did a good job with the horses this morning." She moved closer to the bed. "Thanks for that."

"I didn't have a choice, did I?"

"You know, things don't have to be this hard, Kaitlyn." She thought for a moment, trying to choose her words carefully. "It's not wrong for you to have fun, to be happy."

"Then why are you always telling me *not* to have fun?" Kaitlyn challenged, giving her a stubborn look. "Every time I do something I want to do, you get pissed."

"That's because some of your choices are dangerous, honey. Going off with two boys who are older and bigger than you is not smart. Drinking alcohol leads to bad decisions. You're too young to know the kind of trouble you can get into. I'm trying to protect you."

"Why do you even bother? I'm supposed to be dead."

Her jaw dropped at her niece's words. "Why would you say that?"

"Because it's true. I was in the car. I should have died with them."

She licked her lips, her heart pounding, as she wrestled with the right response. Kaitlyn had said so very, very little about the crash that she didn't want to get this wrong. If her niece was opening up even a bit, it could be a breakthrough.

"Your mom would not want you to be dead, Kaitlyn. She would want you to lead a long and happy life."

"She was mad at me," Kaitlyn murmured, her voice so soft Lizzie could barely hear her.

"Even if she was mad about something, she still loved you."

"You don't know that. You weren't there. You weren't *ever* there. You act like you were so close to my mom, but you weren't. So stop trying to pretend you know anything."

She frowned at another reminder of some estrangement she hadn't even been aware of. "If your mom was angry because we didn't spend enough time together, I'm sorry. I didn't know that. She didn't say anything to me. I loved her."

Kaitlyn gave her a disbelieving look.

She sat down on the bed. "That's the truth, Kaitlyn. After our dad left, Kelly took care of me. My mom worked all the time, and she had other issues with depression and drinking, so sometimes she forgot to make dinner or buy groceries. Kelly was the one who helped me with my homework and made sure I had something to eat. She was only six years older than me, but she was like a mother to me." She drew in a shaky breath. "I miss her, Kaitlyn. I know you do, too. We have that in common. I wish you could see that."

Kaitlyn's eyes glittered with unshed tears, but she

didn't let them fall. She wiped her eyes, then got up from the bed and walked to the door.

"Wait," Lizzie said, feeling like she'd blown it again by talking about Kelly, but maybe she should just be happy that she'd gotten some response out of Kaitlyn, even if it was negative. She rose to her feet. "I really wish you'd come with us on the hike."

"I hate hiking. I'll be at the pool."

She sighed as Kaitlyn left the room. Since her niece hated pretty much everything, it wasn't surprising hiking was on the list.

As she went downstairs, she replayed their conversation in her head, realizing that she had learned one important piece of information, and she probably should have focused on that. Kaitlyn had said her mother was angry with her before she died. It was probably over nothing, just teenage girl stuff, but maybe she needed to find out exactly what it was.

Later, she told herself. She'd go hiking and give Kaitlyn a chance to calm down, and then she would try again.

***

"When did you start hiking?" Brad asked Luke as they waited for the others to gather outside the lodge.

"When I was seven," he replied. "It was here in this valley. My parents used to bring me and my brothers to the resort for family vacation."

"So you've been to Wolmer Falls?"

"No. We went to a waterfall, but that wasn't the name, and it was not very far from here."

"Sweetheart Falls," Brad said with a nod. "It's a half mile behind the lodge. It's not very big, but the little kids love it."

"It seemed big to me at the time," he said with a grin. "Anyway, years later, in my late teens, I climbed Half Dome and about seven years ago, I did El Capitan. I included some of that footage in my first film."

"I remember. You captured the experience perfectly. I've had the pleasure of doing both twice. It never gets old."

"No, it doesn't."

"But you've been all over the world. You've climbed Everest. That's amazing." Brad gave him a sheepish smile. "As you can probably tell, I'm a big fan. You're a rock star to the guys I hang out with."

He laughed. "Trust me, I have met a lot of people far more bad ass than me," he said, genuinely meaning it. "I push the boundaries, but I've filmed people who have never heard of boundaries."

"When is the next film coming out?"

"Hopefully in six weeks to two months. We just shot the last segment. Now it's onto editing."

"And then what?"

He grinned at Brad's enthusiasm. "I have some ideas; we'll see how they develop."

"What ideas are those?" Lizzie asked, joining their conversation.

"For my next film," he said.

"And…" she asked, curiosity in her eyes.

"I can't say yet."

"Sounds mysterious."

"More like I just don't plan that far ahead," he said dryly.

"True. I forgot."

"But I have gotten better," he said, seeing the

gleam in her eyes. "I've had to. I have several corporate sponsorships and contracts to fulfill, which means I need to know where I'm going, what I'm going to be wearing, and who I'm going to be shooting, so there's definitely more advance prep than when I first started out."

"I didn't realize you have sponsors," she said. "I thought only athletes and celebrities have those."

"Apparently, some companies think I qualify."

"He more than qualifies," Brad put in. "Luke is a super athlete, Liz. He does things most people wouldn't dream of doing. Didn't you see the commercial World Sports did with him bungee jumping off the Widow Maker Bridge in New Zealand?"

"No, I didn't see that. And I don't think jumping off a bridge called the Widow Maker sounds like a good idea."

"I survived. Not that I would have made anyone a widow."

"Was it easier to risk your life knowing there wasn't a woman waiting for you to come home?" she asked, her tone more serious than it had been before.

"I think it was," he said slowly. "Although, there were a few women along the way who asked me to live so I could take them to dinner."

"More than a few, I bet. You probably have groupies in addition to sponsors."

He shrugged, happy when the Harrison family joined the group. He didn't really want to talk about other women with Lizzie.

The Harrison family included dad Roger, mom Joanne, daughter Julie, and sons Rex and Will. The boys avoided making eye contact with Luke, which he found amusing. He liked that they were worried about him. Hopefully, that would keep them in line for the rest of their vacation at the resort.

Also joining the group hike was a young newlywed couple, Palmer and Janet, who couldn't seem to stop touching each other, and an older, long-married couple Richard and Madeline, who were visiting Yosemite from the UK, and told the group they were avid hikers. They also appeared to be avid conversationalists, keeping up a steady stream of comments and questions as Brad gave them some initial instructions and then they all made their way to the trail.

He brought up the rear with Lizzie, who'd changed from tennis shoes into hiking boots that looked new enough to still have the price tag on them.

"I can't believe you've been here for six months and haven't broken those in," he told her.

"I've been busy, and hiking isn't at the top of my list."

"What is Kaitlyn doing?"

"Hanging at the pool. I'm actually happy we have the Harrison boys with us."

He smiled. "You talk about those kids the way people used to talk about me and my siblings. We were known in the neighborhood as the Brannigan boys or the Brannigan brothers, sometimes with the word *wild* added in front of the tag."

"You were wild, and those boys are, too."

"Or they're just being boys."

"I wonder if I should tell their parents about the drinking."

"You could, but I'm sure the boys will deny it, and you don't have any proof."

"I guess I'll play it by ear. I wish there was a parenting handbook, somewhere I could go to look up the answers to the millions of questions that I have."

"That would make it too easy."

"Nothing easy about it." She paused. "When we were together, I did envy you your big family. You always had brothers texting you or dropping in for a weekend. It seemed fun. I just had Kelly, who was great, but she was six years older and definitely played the serious big sister card more than a few times."

"James used to do that to me."

"He's the oldest, right?"

"Yeah. And like your sister, James became a surrogate father for all of us when my dad was busy with his businesses. He was often a pain in the ass, but I appreciate his efforts more now."

As the trail narrowed, they moved into single file. He urged Lizzie in front of him because he wanted to look at her as much as he could. The others might be caught up in the wonders of Yosemite, but he couldn't take his eyes off her. Nor could he seem to stop the stream of memories that followed her every step, the sway of her hips reminding him of more intimate moments between them…moments that he wanted again.

She flung him a quick look over her shoulder. "How are you doing back there?"

"Great," he said. "You don't look too unhappy."

"It is nice to be outside." She paused as the group ahead slowed down to maneuver their way around some large boulders. "Today is not my normal kind of workday, and I must admit I'm enjoying the break. What about you?"

"I'm enjoying you," he said, the words coming out before he could stop them.

Surprise and something else flashed through her eyes. "You shouldn't say things like that—not here, not now."

"So later?"

"I didn't say that."

"You only said here and now; that implies later is a possibility."

"When did you get so interested in semantics?" she challenged.

"Since about ten seconds ago," he said with a grin. "Keep moving, Lizzie. We'll talk about all this later."

"Or not," she said, following the group around the rocks.

The hike was an easy one by his standards, although the last mile was somewhat steeper in nature, and there were several narrow places to get through. At one point, Lizzie stumbled over a rock, and he immediately grabbed her arm.

"Okay?" he asked.

"Fine," she said.

He ran his hand down her arm, his fingers latching around hers. She gave him a wary look.

"For safety," he lied.

She didn't look like she believed him, but she left her hand in his, and then he was the one wishing he hadn't made the move. Because he liked holding her hand; he liked walking through nature with her; he liked just being with her.

There was a good chance they could both get burned again—but not now, not today.

Eight

‒‒➤➤◄◄◄‒

They reached the falls thirty minutes later. There were at least a dozen people splashing or swimming in the multiple pools that were fed by the waterfall. The water looked more than a little inviting as the temperature was now in the upper seventies.

Brad handed out his wife's homemade cookies and bottles of cold water from the pack he'd brought, while some of the group stripped down to their bathing suits and jumped in the water.

Lizzie let go of his hand. "I'm going to get my feet wet," she said, kicking off her shoes. She made her way into the water, flinging him a surprised but happy look as she waded in up to her knees. "It's cold," she said.

"I'm not surprised."

"Why don't you come in?"

"I'm okay," he said, as she splashed around in the pool. Lizzie had always liked water. They'd gone to school twenty minutes from the beach, and they'd spent many, many weekends, diving in and out of the surf in Santa Monica.

As he watched her now, he was reminded of the story she'd told him about his parents' first meeting, the way his father had watched his mother skip from rock to rock in the creek, how he couldn't take his eyes off of her, how he knew she was the woman…

He blew out a breath, feeling a strangely deep connection to his dad, one he'd never expected to feel. After his mother died, his father had been all about ambition, making money, buying and selling companies, networking, traveling—anything but being with his family. But before that…before that, his dad had been a husband in love, a father who spent time with his kids, a family man. He just hadn't known how to be that man without his wife.

Kathleen Brannigan had left a big hole in all of their lives, but maybe he'd never appreciated how much his father had loved her until now. Now, in the valley where they'd fallen for each other, he could see it so much more clearly.

Maybe that was the legacy his dad had left him. Maybe it wasn't all about Lizzie.

But as she turned around and gave him a radiant smile that hardened his body and made his heart race, he knew it had a little to do with Lizzie, too. His dad had wanted to throw them back together to see what would happen…

What would happen?

A lot of ideas ran through his mind, most of which involved both of them getting naked and spending a lot of time together in bed.

Damn. Maybe he should go into that cold water and give himself a dose of reality.

"So, Luke," Brad began.

He dragged his gaze away from Lizzie, both relieved and annoyed by the interruption.

"Shari tells me you and Liz used to go out," Brad said, a curious gleam in his eyes.

"A long time ago. It didn't end well."

"Looks like you're getting along okay now."

"Well, Lizzie has good reason to be nice to me since I inherited the resort."

"I don't think it's just that."

He shrugged, not sure what to say to that. He decided to change the subject. "How long have you worked at the resort?"

"Six years. I used to work in the park before that, but then I met Shari. She was a sous chef here for the previous chef. It was love at first sight. We got married the next year, and she became head chef a year later. Then I took over the adventure program. It's been great. We live together and work together, but not too close," he added with a grin. "She does her thing, and I do mine. It's all good. Of course, things will be changing in a month when our daughter comes along. I do not know what I'm going to do with a girl."

"You'll figure it out. Congratulations."

"Thanks. We're excited—terrified."

"Sounds about right."

"I know I shouldn't ask. It's not my place, but if you are going to sell the resort, can you give us a heads-up? I want to make sure I can take care of the family, and both our incomes are tied up here. There aren't a lot of jobs in the valley where we can both work and live."

He saw the concern in Brad's eyes. "Of course. I still haven't decided what I want to do."

"I'm not trying to push you. I know your father

recently died, and I'm sorry. I didn't know him beyond his name, but Lizzie always said she liked him."

He was still surprised his father had never made a trip to the resort after he bought it. He'd obviously had a lot of complicated feelings about the place, and now he'd left Luke to deal with it all. It was strange; he'd never owned anything big except a car, and he'd bought that used. He rented his apartment, his studio time, and a lot of his equipment. He'd never had a deed with his name on it until now, and he just didn't know what to do with it.

"Are you going in the water?" Brad asked, changing the subject.

"I don't think so."

"I'm going to help the Harrisons get some pictures."

He nodded as Brad walked over to Mrs. Harrison and her daughter, who were trying to take a selfie.

He turned his head, seeing Lizzie caught up in conversation with the couple from the UK. She might not have been trained to run a lodge or be a hotel manager, but her friendly warmth made her the perfect hostess. She'd definitely embraced her new life, and he respected that. It couldn't have been easy to give up her dreams, not to mention losing the closest person to her—Kelly. He doubted she'd even had time to really absorb that loss. Kaitlyn's needs had taken all of her focus.

As he looked around the pool, he noticed that the Harrison boys had left the water, put on their shoes, and were moving toward the next trailhead, which would take them onto a much more advanced and treacherous climb toward Last Chance Rock. Brad had made it clear that the hike was ending at these falls, that the trail beyond was narrow, slippery and incredibly dangerous.

He ran after them, not wanting to take a second to chase down Brad or their parents. He grabbed two skinny arms just as the boys were about to enter the trailhead. He yanked them both backward.

"Not happening," he said firmly.

"We were just looking," the older kid Rex said, squirming under his tight grip.

"You can look from here, or better yet, back there with your parents."

"It's fine," Will, the younger one, said. "We'll go back."

"Good, but here's a warning. If I let you go, and you run, I will follow you, and I will catch you, and you will pay. Got it?"

He was answered with two sullen nods.

"And while we're talking," he added. "Do you know how stupid you were last night to be drinking with a thirteen-year-old girl? Use your head before you do something you can't come back from. Now, go back to your parents before I decide to tell them everything you've been up to." He let go of their arms and shoved them down the path toward the pools.

As he followed them back to the group, Lizzie's gaze met his. She waded out of the water. "Everything all right?" she asked.

"Perfect."

"The boys were going to sneak onto the upper trail, weren't they?"

"Looked that way, but I let them know that wasn't happening."

"Thanks. I didn't realize they'd gone up there until you were sending them back. I should have paid more attention."

"Nothing happened."

"But I don't want you to think that we're careless with the customers on these hikes. Brad is a really good guide. He just got caught up talking to Mr. and Mrs. Harrison, and—"

"Stop. I don't think any of that," he said, calming her worries. "It's possible the kids would have turned back as soon as they saw what was in store for them and Brad would have gone after them if I'd let him know. I figured I could handle the situation myself, and I did. So we're good."

"All right. Thanks."

"To be honest, I might have tried the same thing at their age, especially after the story Tom told last night about undiscovered gold."

"I keep telling him we need to rethink that," she said with a laugh as she grabbed her new hiking boots off a rock and sat down to put them on.

"It might be worth considering."

"Would you risk your life for a gold nugget?"

"I've risked it for a lot less."

She finished tying her shoes and then stood up. "Why do you do it, Luke?"

It was a question she'd asked him before—ten years ago. It was a question his family had asked, his sponsors, thousands of reporters around the globe.

Why do you do it? What drives you? Do you have a death wish? What are you trying to prove?

He'd never come up with a good answer.

"Luke," she pressed, her gaze inquisitive. "I really want to know. I asked you before, and you could never tell me."

"Why do you think I can tell you now?"

"Because you've had ten years to think about it."

He tipped his head. "Good point."

"But still no answer?"

"I guess…" His voice trailed away as he looked off to the distant peaks of El Capitan and Half Dome. "I need to push myself. I need to feel…alive. There's always been this feeling that I have to chase, only I never quite catch it."

Her gaze clung to his. "I think that's the most honest you've ever been with me."

"I never lied to you, Lizzie. Maybe I'm just more self-aware now."

"Maybe you are."

He looked into her serious and searching blue eyes and felt like she was stripping him bare and not in the way he wanted. She was getting into his head. She was seeing past his defenses, and why not? He'd just opened himself up in a big way.

"Do you think you'll ever catch the feeling?" she asked him.

He shrugged. "Who knows? It could be I'm just addicted to the adrenaline rush. I'm always looking for the next one."

"Only the next one doesn't satisfy you any more than the one before," she said.

"I wouldn't say that," he hedged.

"You want to know what I think?"

"Probably not," he said warily.

"I don't think you're chasing a feeling…I think you're chasing yourself. You're afraid to be still, afraid you won't be enough if you're not moving, not achieving something, but you are enough, and you don't need to climb a mountain to realize that."

It was probably the most insightful thing anyone

had ever said to him, but it also made him feel defensive. "Being still doesn't get you anywhere. Sometimes it's not enough to sit in a quiet room and plan out your life. You have to go look for it. You have to grab it with both hands and hang on tight."

She stared back at him. "There have to be quiet times. You can't live your life on a dead run."

"Who says you can't? You? Would you have taken this break if Kelly hadn't died? Wouldn't you be walking the fast streets of New York, looking for your next gig, your next moment to be in the spotlight?"

A frown entered her eyes. "I don't know. Perhaps—for a while longer anyway."

"That's where I am. I like my life. I like what I do. Why should I change it?"

"I guess you shouldn't." She let out a breath and looked away from him. "Brad is waving us over. Are you ready to go back?"

He was more than ready to end this conversation, that was for sure. Lizzie had rattled him with her comments, and he'd obviously shaken her up, too. That was the thing. They were both really good at cutting through each other's bullshit. At one point that had seemed like a positive; now…he didn't know.

She'd been having fun until she'd remembered that Luke's life was thousands of miles away from here, and he had no intention of changing it. Which meant that he was no doubt going to destroy her life by selling the resort to some corporation that would install their own staff. Or even if they kept her on for a while, it would probably be temporary.

Worry and annoyance made her walk faster on the way back to the lodge. She could feel Luke's presence behind her, but she didn't look around or speak to him again, and he seemed just as uninterested in talking to her.

Maybe they both needed to do more thinking, less talking.

If he sold the resort, she'd figure something out. It would be another rough change for Kaitlyn, although possibly a welcome one for her niece. But whatever happened, they'd make it.

She just really loved the lodge, the staff, the guests, not to mention the location. It might not have been her first choice of a job, but in some ways she felt like she'd really found a home, people she could count on. At the resort, they all looked out for one another. They were a family and the guests often became friends. She liked the social interaction, the constantly changing dynamics.

Sometimes she missed the music—more than sometimes in truth, but after everything that had happened—the pain of losing Kelly, the difficulty connecting with Kaitlyn, and the abrupt change in her living and working situations—music seemed like the last thing she needed to worry about.

One day she'd play again.

Or not. But either way, she'd survive. She'd always been a survivor. That hadn't changed.

When they reached the resort, the group split up. She didn't know where Luke went. When she turned around, he was gone. It was just as well.

She went to the pool first and saw Kaitlyn sunning herself on a lounger. She was alone, headphones in her ears as usual. Walking over, she sat down on the chair next to her niece and touched her on the arm.

Kaitlyn squinted one eye open and then sighed. She took out her earphones.

"How's it going?" Liz asked.

"Fine."

"Did you get lunch?"

"Yes."

"How is the summer reading coming along?" she asked. Kaitlyn was due to start school on Tuesday and she'd been given a reading list to complete over the summer.

"I'll get it done," she replied, ready to put her headphones back in.

She put a hand on her arm. "Why don't we talk about what you've read later tonight?"

"Why?"

"Because I'm worried you won't get your reading finished and then you'll be behind."

"I said I'll do it. They're stupid easy books."

"Then they shouldn't take you long to get through. You used to love to read. We read *Harry Potter* together when I watched you that week your parents went to London."

"I was nine."

"Kids your age still read."

Kaitlyn shrugged, looking bored with the whole conversation. Then her phone buzzed, and she looked down at a text.

"Who's that?" Liz asked.

"No one."

"Obviously, it's someone."

"You've taken me away from all my friends. Isn't that enough for you?"

"I don't think those friends were very good for you."

Kaitlyn didn't bother to answer, her attention on her phone as her fingers flew over the keypad.

"I'm going to be in my office," she said, giving up. "I'll see you at dinner."

No answer. She sighed and got to her feet, then headed back into the lodge.

She worked in her office for the next hour, going over the staffing schedule. The part-time summer help would be gone after Monday as they settled into a quieter time of the year. She also went over the books and then reviewed the notes she'd made in preparation for a pitch to Colin Brannigan about repairs and improvements.

She felt a little sad thinking that Colin was gone. She'd been so focused on what his death meant to her that she felt guilty for not grieving him in the proper way. He had been more than a boss to her. She hadn't known him well, but he'd been Luke's father, and he'd saved her ass by giving her the job without any experience. For some reason he'd believed in her, and he'd told her that he liked to bet on the underdog.

She just wished he'd bet a little more on his son. She thought Luke's wandering ways and his need to chase something had to do with his father's absence in his life as well as his mother's death. He'd been close to his brothers, but there had been so many of them, and Luke, at heart, was kind of a loner. He could be funny and loud and the life of the party, but then there were the times when he just wanted to think and ponder, walk and hike, study the stars and contemplate life. That was the Luke she actually loved the most. That was the guy she'd given her heart to.

He might not think he liked to be still, but she knew he did.

The door to her office opened, and her pulse jumped. But it wasn't Luke who entered the room; it was Brad.

"Sorry about what happened earlier," he told her. "I should have figured those boys would try to sneak away. I'm usually better at spotting the troublemakers."

"Their parents distracted you."

"Still, it's my responsibility, and I know you want to make a good impression on Luke."

"I don't think what happened today will influence his decision in any way."

"Well, that's good." Brad paused. "I also wanted to talk to you about Shari. She won't like me butting into her business, but I'm worried that she's working too much. I know she's going to cut back after the weekend, but we still don't have a replacement chef, and she seems really tired lately."

"I talked to her about it earlier. She knows we need her input on the chef search, and she's been very slow to give it. Frankly, I don't think she knows what to do with herself if she's not in the kitchen."

"I get it. But I want her off her feet a bit more."

"I will try to make that happen. "

"I know you have a lot on your plate now that Colin has passed away."

"I can handle it."

"I hope Luke leaves things the way they are. I asked him to give us a heads-up if he's going to sell. We all don't just work here; many of us live here, too."

"I don't think he'll shut us down without notice,"

she said. "He's not that kind of man."

Brad cocked his head to the right. "Is he the kind of man you might give a second chance to?"

She sucked in a quick breath at the question. "I— why would you ask that?"

"I saw him holding your hand. You looked good together."

"I tripped. He helped me up."

Brad grinned. "And that's the story you're sticking to?"

"That's the one."

Brad walked to the door. "We're going to show Luke's latest movie in the living room at eight tonight. I've told all the guests. Shari is going to make three different kinds of popcorn, for what reason, I do not know, but it's happening."

"Really? I didn't know about that."

"You don't mind, do you? It's movie night."

"Does Luke know?"

"I just ran it past him. He said he'd come."

"Okay, then I guess that will work."

"Good." Brad paused. "For what it's worth, Liz, I don't think he's over you. So if you're not over him…"

Brad gave her a second to answer. When she didn't respond, he left.

The door was almost closed when she finally got the words out. "I am over him."

But there was no one there to hear her vow. Just as well, because she wasn't sure she believed her own words.

Nine

⇒⇒⇒≪≪≪

Almost twenty people, including guests and staff members, showed up in the living room for Luke's movie. They had set up a player to stream movies to a big screen on the wall, with cozy couches and armchairs arranged for comfortable seating. Shari had put out not only several varieties of popcorn but also brownies, a fruit plate, and pitchers of lemonade.

Liz had gotten Kaitlyn to come, and she was sitting next to Julie Harrison, looking probably as happy as Liz had seen her in a while. She just needed to make sure that when the lights went out, Kaitlyn didn't disappear with the boys.

Before starting the movie, Brad introduced Luke and asked him if he wanted to say a few words.

Luke stepped to the front of the room, and Liz couldn't help the little thrill that ran down her spine. He'd changed out of jeans and T-shirt and wore slacks and a button-down shirt tonight. His beard was neatly trimmed and his handsome face and dark-brown eyes compelled the attention of everyone, including her.

"The movie you're about to see," Luke said, "was shot across five continents and ten countries. The people you'll meet are just like you. They might not speak your language, but they're living their lives just as you do: working jobs, going to school, raising families, and struggling to find meaning in their worlds. On their days off, they pursue passions that push them to the limits. Why do they do this?" He paused for a moment. "It's because they're afraid."

Goose bumps ran down her arms at his words. *Was he talking about the people in the film or about himself?*

"You might not believe that they're afraid when you watch them clinging to the face of a sheer rock wall thousands of feet above the ground or launching themselves out of a plane," Luke continued. "But they are. It's just not what you think of as fear. They're not afraid of falling or even of dying. Well, maybe some are, if they're smart," he added with a laugh. "But what they're really afraid of is that they'll let fear stop them from reaching for the stars. It's fear that they won't try hard enough to live up to their potential, to try as much as they can, to experience everything a human being can feel. You'll see amazing stories, and not all of them are triumphant, but we learn as much, if not more, from the failures. I hope you enjoy taking the journey with them as much as I did."

Luke's words resonated deep within her. Luke wasn't just chasing something he couldn't quite catch; he was worried that he wouldn't live hard enough, wouldn't be all that he was supposed to be. But would he ever feel satisfied with what he'd already done, the amazing things he'd accomplished so far?

She really hoped so.

Luke stood against the back wall as the movie played. She was acutely aware of his presence for the first few minutes, but then she got caught up in the storylines. Luke didn't just show himself and other thrill seekers jumping off cliffs; he started on a more personal level. He showed them at work, at home with their families. He talked to them about their dreams, their fears, their flaws. Sometimes he went with them on their adventures, a participant as well as a cameraman. Other times, he hung back; he let them have their own moment to succeed or fail.

As the film played, she experienced as many emotions as the people she was watching and judging by the entranced silence in the room, she wasn't alone. When the lights came on, she felt as exhausted and exhilarated as the climbers reaching the summit of Mt. Everest.

Luke was immediately swarmed with people offering amazed thanks and congratulations.

Liz was happy to see that Kaitlyn and the boys had stayed, although she realized she'd been so caught up in the movie she probably wouldn't have seen them leave.

Shari came up next to her. "So, can I just say wow? That man is a super stud. And you let him go?"

"It seemed like a good idea at the time," she said with a wistful sigh. "But now, I can't even remember why I thought that."

"Maybe he's improved with age," Shari said with a smile.

"I think he definitely has."

"I'm going to head up to bed, but before I go I wanted to ask you about tomorrow—about Kelly's birthday. How do you want to handle that with

Kaitlyn? Do we talk about it? Do we ignore it? Do we celebrate? I don't know what the right thing is to do."

Looking into Shari's troubled eyes, Liz didn't know, either. "I feel like whatever we do it will be the wrong thing. I think we just need to follow Kaitlyn's lead."

"So we're ignoring it."

"I think so. Lately when I bring up Kelly, Kaitlyn goes on attack, telling me I was a bad sister… I know anger is a normal part of the grieving process, but how long does it go on?"

Shari gave her a sympathetic smile. "As long as it does."

"That's not helpful."

"I don't have any easy answers; I wish I did. Watching what you've been going through with Kaitlyn is making me worry about what's in store for me with this baby. You never think about what your child is going to be like at thirteen."

Liz smiled. "You have plenty of years to get through before then. And you'll be a great mom. I have no doubt about that."

"You're doing a good job, too, Liz. You've been a stand-in mother for six months, so give yourself a break. Deep down Kaitlyn loves you, even if right now she's not willing to show you."

"I love her, too, even when she's making it really, really hard." She paused. "Go, get some rest. And tomorrow we amp up the search for a new chef."

"I'm ahead of you. I have someone coming in tomorrow morning to work with me through the weekend. Her name is Val Marlow, and she has excellent references. She's been a sous chef in San Francisco for five years. Most importantly, her boyfriend is now working in Yosemite, so she's looking to relocate to this area, and a job here would be great for her."

"I'm so happy to hear this. You know your job will be waiting for you when you're ready to come back, but I think taking a few months for yourself and the baby is important."

"I know. I just hate anyone else running my kitchen."

"It's still your kitchen."

"For a while anyway, until Luke makes his decision."

"Don't worry about that tonight."

"I won't, because I know you're worrying for me and for all of us. Good-night, Liz."

"Sleep well," she said.

She walked over to Luke, who was talking to Tina.

"This guy is amazing," Tina said with the same look of wonder most people wore after talking to Luke and hearing about his adventures."

"I know," she said. She glanced past Luke at Kaitlyn, who had gotten up from the couch but was texting on her phone. "Kaitlyn, what did you think of the movie?"

Kaitlyn didn't answer.

"Kaitlyn," she said more sharply.

"It was all right. Must be nice to do whatever you want to do, go wherever you want to go," she said to Luke, resentment in her tone.

"You'll get there," Luke said.

"No I won't. I'm not rich, and I don't have parents to help me get anywhere."

Liz felt like she'd taken a knife to the heart at

Kaitlyn's words. She wanted to say she was here, she would help, she would do whatever she could to make Kaitlyn's life happy, but her niece wasn't interested in anything she had to say.

"I got myself everywhere I wanted to go," Luke told Kaitlyn. "And I worked for it. Nobody handed me anything."

"Whatever. I'm going to bed."

Liz watched Kaitlyn make her way to the stairs, hoping that her niece truly was going to bed and had no intention of sneaking out with the Harrison boys again.

"Don't worry," Luke said. I talked to Roger Harrison earlier. I told him he might want to keep an eye on the boys. He said he was already on it. I guess the younger brother's guilt got the best of him, and he confessed they'd taken a bottle of alcohol from the parents' cooler and tried to share it with Kaitlyn. Roger said the boys would not be going anywhere tonight."

"That's a relief. I thought you weren't going to rat them out?"

"The opportunity arose, so I took it."

"I appreciate it. I'll sleep better knowing Kaitlyn isn't going to sneak out on me."

He folded his arms across his chest, giving her a speculative look.

"What?" she asked, feeling a little nervous all of a sudden.

"Do you want to get some air? I hear there's a rooftop patio with a great view of the stars."

She really should say no. No good could come of sharing a moonlit, starry night with Luke, but as her stomach twisted, her nerves tingled, and her heart beat faster, she became a prisoner of her own desire. Luke would leave. But he was here now, and she didn't want to just say good-night and go to bed.

"Let's go," she said, leading the way up to the roof.

There was a long bench on the flat roof, providing an excellent view of the starry sky.

Luke sat down and stretched out his legs as he directed his gaze upwards. He let out a sigh. "This is good."

She sat down next to him and looked up at the brightly lit sky as well. "A lot of stars out tonight."

He took her hand, and she jumped, but she didn't pull away, because the warmth of his fingers sent a wave of heat through her.

"What did you think of my movie, Lizzie?" Luke asked.

As she looked into his eyes, she sensed there was a lot behind the lightly spoken question. "I loved it."

"You can be honest."

"I am being honest. You took me along on every adventure. I felt exhausted by the end of it but also exhilarated, like I'd climbed the mountain with you, only I wasn't freezing or starving or trying to stay upright on exhausted legs."

He smiled. "That's the reaction I was hoping for."

"You got it. I now completely understand why you're a superstar," she added with a smile. "And I'm not surprised. When you first talked about making movies like that, you were so passionate and excited and determined. I didn't know they would turn out this good, and I certainly didn't know how many chances you would take with your own life, but I always knew you'd do something incredible with your life. I was right."

"Thanks."

"I liked your speech, too. It was interesting how you spoke about the people in your film, how you made them real."

"They were real people, same as you and me."

"I wouldn't have seen them that way if you hadn't showed me. It's easier to look at superstars as people born with very special talents or blessed with some unusual strength, but not the guy driving the garbage truck in the morning so he can be home to pick up his kid from kindergarten at noon."

"I believe that ordinary people are capable of doing extraordinary things. The courage is there within them; they just have to find it."

"You make it sound so easy."

"It's not easy, but it's possible. You've done it. You found the courage to walk out on the stage and play for the toughest critics in the world. You found the courage to give up your life and raise your niece. Hell, you found the courage to walk away from me when you needed to."

"I thought you hated me for that."

"I did for a long time, but that's only because…I loved you so much."

She sucked in a quick breath. "I feel like we're veering into dangerous territory."

He smiled and squeezed her fingers. "And I feel like we haven't missed a beat. All those years in between are gone. It's you and me again. I like talking to you, Lizzie. I always did."

"You liked to do more than talk," she teased.

"Guilty. But when we weren't doing that, talking was good."

"It was good." She swallowed as a knot of emotion began to grow in her throat. "I deliberately didn't watch any of your movies before tonight. I didn't think I could stand seeing you. I thought it would hurt too much."

"Are you hurting now?"

"A little," she admitted. "I can't help thinking about all the adventures I missed. Not that I would have wanted to participate in most of what you've done, but I would have loved to see some of the places you've been."

"There's still time."

"I wish that were true. But I have even less of a chance now of traveling the world…I have Kaitlyn. I have roots. I can't take off and go where I want. I had my chance; I didn't take it."

He stared back at her. "What if I gave you another chance?"

"Why would you?" she asked, as her blood rushed through her veins at the intense look of desire in his eyes.

"Because I want you, Lizzie."

She wanted to ask why, for what, for how long…but she couldn't get any words out.

He leaned forward and pushed a strand of her hair off her forehead, then let his fingers slide down her cheek. "You are so beautiful, even prettier than I remember. You always had the softest lips, the sweetest sigh. I want those lips; I want that sigh."

Her heart pounded against her chest. "We—can't."

"Can't we?" he countered. "Who's going to stop us?"

"One of us should probably do that."

"You don't think it's going to be me, do you?"

She knew it wasn't going to be him; she was also afraid it wouldn't be her. "Oh, Luke," she said, giving him that sigh he wanted. "I could never say no to you."

"You did once."

"It was the hardest thing I ever did. I'm sorry I hurt you."

"I'm sorry, too." He leaned in and took the kiss he wanted.

She opened her mouth to his, sinking into the kiss as heat and passion swept through her. He tasted like Luke: sexy, powerful, and cocky. Oh, how she'd missed him. When it came to making love, he'd always been intense and overwhelming and absolutely perfect.

His tongue tangled with hers as his arms wrapped around her back, pulling her up against his body—a body fit and lean and so very male. She wanted to touch every inch of him and then follow with her mouth.

She ran her hands up under his shirt, hearing his breath quicken as she ran her fingers across his abs.

And this time it was Luke who sighed, a needy groan that only intensified the heat between them.

Kissing wasn't enough. She wanted him the way he wanted her and that did not involve clothes.

"Your room," he muttered, lifting his mouth from hers long enough to ask the question. "Where is it?"

"Downstairs," she said breathlessly. "But Kaitlyn—we share the apartment."

"I have a cabin. It's not that far."

It was far enough away to give her time to catch her breath, change her mind. So she said yes, thinking she still had time to say no…if she really wanted to.

"Yes," she whispered.

"Thank God." He jumped to his feet, pulling her up along with him.

They went down the stairs and through the front door of the lodge. Fortunately, they didn't run into anyone on their way to Luke's cabin.

She was a little surprised when Luke fumbled with the key, but it was that slight shake in his hand that took away whatever lingering doubts she might have had. This was Luke—her first love—really, her only love. If they had one more night together, she'd take it.

Luke got the door open and pulled her inside, kicking it shut behind him. He didn't bother with the lights and the streaming glow from the moon and the stars through the windows was even more romantic. She didn't want to see the cabin; she just wanted to see him, to be with him.

Now that she'd gotten past her indecision, she was all in, impatient and filled with desire to be with him. She went in for a kiss, throwing her arms around his neck, pulling his head down to hers.

Their panting, breathless kisses were punctuated by the removal of their clothes. She took off his shirt. He returned the favor, taking the time to unhook her bra as well. As she slipped the straps off her shoulders, he lowered his head and kissed her breasts, swirling his tongue around her already hardened nipples.

It had been so long since she had felt his mouth, since she'd felt so needy, so desperate for a man.

Her hands moved to his jeans, feeling the impressive bulge that told her just how needy and desperate he was, too.

She wanted to get those pants off him as fast as she could. She pulled open the snap and unzipped. He pushed his jeans and briefs over his ass and down his legs, kicking his way out of them. Then he helped her out of her jeans.

Finally, they were naked, and she couldn't help but take a second to appreciate the male in front of her. She wanted to soak in the sight of him, because there was a part of her that thought this moment wouldn't last nearly long enough.

Luke reached for her, his hands settling on her hips as he backed her toward the bed, and then they tumbled onto the soft mattress together. His mouth and hands were everywhere.

"Wait," she said, putting a hand against his hard chest, her cautious brain still working somewhat.

"You're not changing your mind, are you?" he asked in shock.

"No. But we need protection."

"Right. Hang on."

He got up from the bed and walked into the adjoining bathroom, and she had to admit she enjoyed the view.

She heard him rustling around. "Any luck?"

He came back into the room with a rather triumphant smile, holding two condoms in his hand. He tossed them onto the bedside table, as he settled down next to her with a smile. He kissed her as his hand settled on her breast. "We have two chances to get this right, Lizzie."

"That seems appropriate," she murmured, as she pulled him down on top of her. She loved the feel of his weight on her, the way their bodies came together so naturally. It was as if not a second had passed between this time and the last time.

Luke gave her another long kiss, then made his way slowly down her body until every nerve ending was strumming a song that was all him. Luke liked to go fast in every other part of his life, but not this. With love, he'd always been tormentingly slow, making sure she was as ready as he was, and damn if he didn't still know how to touch her better than anyone else.

And she knew how to touch him, too. She pushed him onto his back and took the same tantalizing journey across his chest before they finally stopped teasing and playing and settled into a rhythm that was all theirs. It was exciting, amazing, fulfilling...and terrifying.

How was she ever going to love anyone but him?

Luke couldn't let go of Lizzie. They'd made love for hours, exploring each other's bodies as if they'd never been there before. And as the dawn light streamed through a parted curtain, he wanted her again. He felt like he was twenty: impatient, insatiable, and crazy about her. The last thing he wanted to do was get out of this bed.

Lizzie snuggled against him, her eyes closed, her cheeks touched with pink, her silky blonde hair tangled from his fingers. He loved looking at her—the sweep of her dark lashes, the fullness of her soft lips.

He drew in a deep breath, realizing he needed to exercise a little self-control, but where Lizzie was concerned, that had always been difficult. He'd never felt like he could get enough of her, and that hadn't changed.

But what now?

Normally, he didn't worry about the morning, about the next day or the next week or the next month, but being with Lizzie wasn't normal. Walking away from her...saying good-bye—how the hell could he do that again?

He groaned and rolled onto his back, staring at the ceiling, his mind going back ten years.

Waiting for her to show up at the airport, he'd paced back and forth in front of the terminal. He'd texted her, called her, imagined the worst when she didn't answer. When he hadn't heard from her twenty-four hours later, he'd called her mother, and she'd told him that Lizzie was fine, but she'd decided to stay in town for the summer. She didn't know why Lizzie hadn't told him that; he didn't know why, either.

He'd gotten on the next plane. He'd spent years burning off his anger and heartbreak. He'd told himself he was better off without her. He'd put all his energy, all his focus into his work, into his adventures. It had paid off on the career front, but personally...

He thought he'd forgotten her, gotten over her...

"Luke?" Her soft, questioning voice brought him back to reality. "What are you thinking about?"

He turned back onto his side, hiding his thoughts behind a smile. "You." He touched her lips. "This mouth."

She grabbed his arm. "We can't start that up again. It's morning."

"So?"

"So, we can't." She gave him a thoughtful look. "That wasn't really what you were thinking about, was it?"

"It doesn't matter."

"I think it might."

"Just remembering the way we were," he admitted.

She nodded, understanding in her eyes. "How can it feel like we were together yesterday instead of ten years ago?"

"I don't know, but it does feel that way."

She put her arm across his waist. "You were remembering our breakup. That's why there were shadows in your eyes. I hurt you."

"You did, but in some ways the anger drove me. I was determined to prove that you'd made a mistake by not sticking by me."

"You've been very successful."

"So have you. I'm proud of you, Lizzie. You set your goals, and you reached them." He paused. "But I think I'm even more impressed by your willingness to take on the incredibly huge and important task of raising your niece. You've changed your entire life around. You forged a new frontier, with a lot of guts."

She bit down on her lips, her eyes blurring with tears. "That means a lot coming from a man who forges new frontiers every day."

"Sometimes a simple choice to move or change jobs is just as big as jumping off of a mountain."

"I wouldn't tell your fans that," she said lightly.

"I think they would understand, because that's the real message of my movies. It's about finding the strength within. Fighting the fear. Being everything you were meant to be."

"You've always had a lot more depth than people realize, Luke."

That was probably true, but she'd always seen

him. That's why it had been so painful when she left. He'd missed her understanding, her counsel, her laugh, her kiss—so many things…They'd had so much more than just physical attraction; they'd had real love. He hadn't even really realized that until just this second.

"I'm proud of you, too, Luke," she said, interrupting his thoughts. "You inspire people and in a world that can be far too cynical, that is worth a lot." She drew in a breath and let it out. "I just…don't know where we go from here."

"Maybe breakfast?" he said lightly.

"You know what I mean."

"We don't have to decide right now. There's a lot to think about."

"More for you than for me," she said. "But you're right. And today isn't the best day for decisions anyway."

He frowned at her words, seeing new shadows fill her eyes. "Why? What's today?"

"It would have been my sister's thirty-sixth birthday."

"I'm sorry." He leaned over and kissed her. "I know the focus is all on Kaitlyn, but you lost your sister, and I know how much you loved her."

"I did love her, but I can't talk about her, because it bothers Kaitlyn."

"I know that feeling. I always wanted to talk about my mom, but my dad didn't want to hear it. We all grieve in different ways."

"I try to remember that. But lately Kaitlyn's anger and her accusations that Kelly's and my relationship wasn't what I remember have been making me a little crazy. I'm afraid one of these days I'm going to snap at her and say something that will only set her back or make any relationship between us impossible."

"I don't think you'll do that. You have too much love for the kid, even when she's yanking your chain."

"I hope you're right about that. Shari and I were thinking of doing something in Kelly's honor today, making my sister's favorite meal, but we're afraid of how Kaitlyn will react. Maybe reminding her that her mom isn't here on what would have been her birthday isn't a good idea."

"It might not be," he said frankly. "You might need to have your own personal celebration and not involve Kaitlyn."

She sighed. "You always tell me the truth, Luke, even when I don't want to hear it. That used to annoy me, but I found I missed it over the years."

"The hard truth has saved my life a few times. I live by it."

"I should go back to the house before Kaitlyn gets up. I need to take a shower and get dressed."

He wasn't quite ready to let her go. "Why don't we take a shower here together?"

"You know where that will lead, and we don't have any more protection."

"We'll improvise. I have a few ideas."

Her blue eyes sparkled as she laughed. "I bet you do."

He grinned back at her. "Is that a yes? I promise to make it worth your while."

"Do you even have to ask?" she returned, as he rolled out of bed and pulled her along with him.

Ten

_⟶≫✦≪⟵_

After the most exciting shower of her life in the past decade, Lizzie went back to the lodge, changed her clothes and checked in on Kaitlyn a little before nine. Her niece was still asleep and actually looked like the angel she'd once been.

She watched Kaitlyn sleep for a few minutes, wishing she could find a way to give her niece the same sense of peace and happiness when she was awake.

Time, she told herself. It was all she had to work with.

Gently closing the door, she went downstairs to the kitchen. Shari introduced her to Val, the auditioning chef, who could hopefully take over when Shari went on maternity leave. Lizzie didn't want to interrupt, so she made herself a bowl of oatmeal and took it into her office.

She fired up her computer, answered emails while she ate, and when she was done, she made her way out to the front desk where Tina was checking in a family of four, excited to get started on their holiday weekend in the mountains.

It was going to be a busy few days, and she was thrilled with that. She wanted Luke to see the resort in full swing.

Kaitlyn got up around ten, unwillingly helped Shari with breakfast cleanup in the kitchen for an hour, then said she was going to the pool. She had nothing to say to anyone and seemed in an intensely bad mood, so Lizzie couldn't bring herself to talk about Kelly's birthday. She should probably just heed Luke's advice and let the day go without mention. Judging by Kaitlyn's demeanor, she was already very aware of the significance of the day.

So she focused on work for the next few hours, keeping busy with new arrivals and signing up guests for the various weekend activities.

As busy as she was, she had to admit she also kept looking for Luke, but she had no idea what he was up to, and she didn't have time to find out.

Maybe he was sleeping, she thought a little after one when she found time to grab a salad. She was happily tired from their sleepless night, and wouldn't have minded a little nap, but there was no time for that.

After her lunch, she decided to look for Kaitlyn to see if she could get her interested in one of the group activities later in the day. Several more young teenagers had checked in earlier in the day with their families, all girls, which Lizzie was happy about, and they were going to do an afternoon trail ride with Tom. Maybe she could find a way to talk Kaitlyn into joining the group. While her niece had made it clear she preferred to be left on her own, Lizzie didn't think it was a good day for solitude and too much thinking.

When she got to the pool, she saw the Harrison boys and their sister Julie, as well as a few other guests, but no Kaitlyn. She walked over to talk to them.

"Hi there. Have you guys seen Kaitlyn?"

Julie shook her head, but the boys exchanged a quick look before saying no.

Her gaze narrowed on the younger one's slightly guilty face. "What aren't you telling me?" she asked.

"She didn't want us to tell you," Will replied.

"Which is exactly why you're going to tell me. Or we can go talk to your parents if you want."

"You are the worst liar," Rex told his younger brother with disgust.

"She said she was going for a hike," Will said. "She wanted to know where the trail started for the falls, so we showed her."

Unease ran through her at that comment. Kaitlyn had shown absolutely no interest whatsoever in going to the falls the entire time they'd been at the resort. In fact, she'd refused to venture into the woods at all.

"By herself?" she asked.

"I didn't see anyone with her," Will said.

"Did she ask you guys to go with her?"

"Nope," Rex answered.

"When was this?"

"An hour or so ago."

"Okay, thanks. If you see her, can you tell her to find me?"

"Sure," Will said.

She walked back to the lodge, a bad, scary feeling building up inside of her. She was so preoccupied she ran straight into Luke when she entered the lobby.

He caught her by the arms. "Whoa. Where's the fire?"

"I'm not sure."

His eyes immediately filled with concern. "What's wrong?"

"I don't know yet. Maybe nothing. Maybe something. I need to find Kaitlyn. The Harrison boys said she asked them how to get to the trail for the falls." She broke away from Luke and jogged up the stairs, hoping that Kaitlyn was actually in her room and had changed her mind about taking a hike.

"Seriously?" Luke asked, close on her heels as they moved down the hall. "I thought she didn't like hiking."

"She hates it." She threw open the door to Kaitlyn's bedroom. Her niece wasn't there, but when she saw what was on the bed, her heart skipped a beat.

An open photo album and several loose pictures were spread across the bed.

She picked up the nearest picture, a family photo from a year ago: Kaitlyn with Kelly and Brian at Disneyland. They were all wearing Mickey Mouse ears on their heads. They were laughing. They were happy.

Her heart broke at the sight of her sister's face, the family she'd created, the love so obvious between all three of them. Her eyes watered, and she couldn't stop the tears from falling.

Luke came up behind her, putting his arms around her. She leaned back against him, needing the comfort, the security of his embrace. But she knew she could only linger there a second. Something was wrong. Kaitlyn had made a decision to do something.

"She must have been looking at these pictures

because it's her mom's birthday," she murmured. "I couldn't get her to go near the albums before this. In fact, I caught her trying to throw them away a few months ago, and I stopped her. I hid them in my closet so she wouldn't be bothered by their presence. But today she must have gone in there and gotten them."

"It could be a good thing," he muttered. "Maybe she just wanted to go for a walk."

"I don't know." As she closed the photo album, she saw one of the lodge brochures on the bed. This particular flyer outlined the hiking trails and on the back was the story of the upper and lower Wolmer Falls, Last Chance Rock and undiscovered gold.

"Oh, my God," she murmured, a sudden surge of adrenaline rushing through her. "She's going up there. She's going to Last Chance Rock. She's going to look for the gold."

"Hold on," Luke said. "You don't know that. She could just be walking up to the lower falls. That's an easy hike. She won't go any farther on her own. She'd be too scared."

"Would she be too scared? She's reckless and angry and sad. That's a terrible combination. I need to find her. I think Brad is in the office. He'll know the way."

"I'll go with you," Luke said, following her down the stairs.

She nodded, happy to take all the help she could get.

Brad was in the office as she'd hoped. He got to his feet, obviously seeing the fear on her face. "What's happened?"

"I think Kaitlyn has gone up to Last Chance Rock and the upper falls on her own," she said.

His jaw dropped. "What? Why would she do that?"

"It's a long story. We need to go after her."

"Of course. We can leave right now. But if you really think she's going past the lower falls, I need to get some supplies. The upper trail is slick and dangerous right now with the upper falls so strong and powerful at this time of the year."

His words only increased her fear. "Get what you need, but make it fast."

Brad had barely moved around the desk when Shari appeared in the doorway. Lizzie could immediately see that something was wrong. Shari's skin was very pale, her eyes wide and worried, and she had a hand on her belly.

Brad rushed to his wife's side. "What is it?" he asked.

"My water broke," she said. "I'm having contractions, but it's too early. I'm supposed to have four more weeks. I can't have a baby now."

"It looks like you don't have a choice," Brad said. He flung a troubled look at Lizzie. "I need to take Shari to the hospital. I—I don't know what to do."

"Yes, you do," she said, wishing that weren't the case but Brad couldn't be in two places at once.

"What else is wrong?" Shari asked, looking from her husband to Liz.

"Kaitlyn has gone missing," she replied. "I think she's on her way up to Last Chance Rock. The flyer was on her bed next to photos of her mom and dad."

"Oh, no." Shari frowned. "What about John? Can he go with you?" she asked, referring to their other rock-climbing guide.

"He took a group up to Paradise Peak this

morning," Brad answered. "He won't be back for hours."

"I'll go look for Kaitlyn," Luke interrupted. "I can make it up any mountain, no sweat."

"Of course you can," Brad said with relief. "Sorry, I wasn't even thinking. I have a pack that's ready to go. It's in the closet down the hall. It should have what you need."

"We'll find it," she said. "You and Shari need to go to the hospital and have your beautiful baby."

"I'm so sorry, Liz," Shari said. "I should have made sure Val was ready to go before now. I think she'll be okay today, but I don't know. I'm leaving you in a bad spot."

She was so worried about Kaitlyn, the fact that she had only a substitute cook at the moment was the least of her problems. "It will be fine. We will manage. You don't worry about anything."

She helped Shari outside while Brad brought the car around.

Once they were headed down the road, Luke appeared at her side with Brad's pack of climbing gear.

"We're good to go," he said. "You need to come with me, Lizzie, at least part of the way. Kaitlyn may need you to talk her down from something."

"I doubt she'd listen to me, but of course I'm going with you. I'll put on my boots. Can you tell Tom and whoever else you can find on the staff to keep an eye out for Kaitlyn?"

"I will." He caught her by the arm as she moved toward the door and gave her a determined look. "It's going to be all right."

She really wanted to believe him. "I hope so. I

can't lose Kaitlyn, too."

"I'm not going to let that happen."

She had never appreciated his confidence more than she did at this moment.

———»»««—

They reached lower Wolmer Falls at half-past three. Lizzie's hope that she'd find Kaitlyn sunning on a rock or swimming in one of the pools was dashed. There was no sign of her niece.

She asked several families in the area if they'd seen Kaitlyn, pulling out her phone to show them a photo, but she struck out until she got to a young guy who said he'd seen her heading for the upper trail an hour earlier. He thought he'd seen an older guy a dozen feet ahead of her; he'd assumed the man was her father.

She didn't like that Kaitlyn had gone past the falls or that there was some unknown random man ahead of her on the trail.

Luke must have seen the panic in her eyes, because he put both hands on her shoulders. "Don't get ahead of yourself. One step at a time. That's how we do this."

"I can't help it. She might act like she's twenty, but she's only thirteen, Luke. She has no common sense, and she's being incredibly reckless."

"We'll find her. And I don't think she has no common sense. There's a good chance when things get too tricky that she'll turn around."

Liz wasn't sure of that at all, not the way Kaitlyn was feeling these days, but they were wasting time talking. "Let's go."

"Okay, I'll lead the way. If you need to rest, let me know. I've got extra waters in my pack."

She nodded, sticking close to Luke as they started up the trail. The first twenty minutes weren't too bad, but just as she was starting to relax, the trail took a turn and the incline in front of her was steep and narrow. On one side was the mountain. On the other was a drop of at least thirty to forty feet and, judging by where they were going, that distance to fall was only going to get greater.

"Don't look down," Luke called back to her, as if he were reading her mind.

"Easy for you to say," she muttered.

"Just focus on your next step."

It was all she could do, or terror would take over. Luke obviously had no concerns at all. He moved with confident agility, occasionally pausing to help her navigate a slippery part of the trail.

For the next twenty minutes, they didn't pass anyone going down, and she couldn't see anyone behind them. It was after four now, but thankfully they still had a few hours of daylight yet. She just hoped they could get to the top, find Kaitlyn, and return to the resort before dark.

The farther they walked, the more she wondered if Kaitlyn really would have done all this by herself. Had she really come this far? Wouldn't fear have forced her to turn around?

Or was it survivor guilt that drove her? She was alive and her parents weren't. She'd told Lizzie that she was supposed to be dead, too. Was this some sort of a suicidal hike? God, she hoped not!

Luke stopped as a heavy log blocked their path. To go around it, they'd have to get very near the edge of the trail and climb over some rather large boulders. One wrong step and they'd tumble over the edge of a sheer rock wall.

"I think if we go across there, we'll be okay," he said, pointing to a spot not far from the edge of the trail.

"She can't have gone past this point," she protested.

"According to the map Brad had in the pack, Last Chance Rock is another quarter mile down the trail. I don't think she'd stop before that."

"What if she's not even up here? What if she's back at the resort?"

"If she were, someone would have texted or called you."

She pulled out her phone. "I only have a weak signal."

"If you want to wait here, I can go ahead on my own."

She didn't think she'd feel any safer standing on this narrow path by herself than going with Luke. "No, I'll keep going."

He nodded approvingly. "Just follow in my footsteps."

They maneuvered around the log, and she breathed a sigh of relief as they made it back onto a wider trail.

Fifteen minutes later, their path was blocked by an enormous boulder standing well over ten feet tall and ten feet wide. Around the right side was a three-foot narrow opening. What was on the other side of that rock was impossible to see.

What she also couldn't see was any sign of Kaitlyn.

"Decision time," Luke said, his lips set in a grim line. "This is Last Chance Rock. We turn around, or we keep going, or I keep going. You have three choices."

"Brad said he did the trail beyond this point only once, and he had to use ropes and picks. We're not prepared for that, are we?"

"There's rope in the pack," he said.

She frowned. "But Kaitlyn doesn't have any of those items. She'd be terrified to go past that rock. I think she went somewhere else. I think she went back."

Did she really believe that or was terror blinding her?

"What do you want to do, Lizzie?" Luke asked. "It's your call."

She drew in a breath. She'd never forgive herself if she turned around and went back to the resort and Kaitlyn wasn't there.

"Let's go a little farther, at least through the opening," she decided. "Maybe it's not as bad as everyone says."

He nodded and moved quickly down the path. He slipped through first, then took her hand, as she made her way between the boulder and the cliff. On the other side, the hillside was rocky and very wet. She could hear the thunder of the distant falls and feel the misting spray on her face. This side of the boulder was also darker and filled with more shadows, the mountain blocking most of the afternoon sun.

In front of her, she saw nothing but terrifying desolation, and she couldn't imagine Kaitlyn on this path alone. But then she saw something on the ground, a shiny silver chain, and her heart stopped.

"Look," she said, pointing to the necklace. "I think that's Kaitlyn's."

Luke moved forward to grab the piece of jewelry. He brought it back to her, and she closed her fingers around the silver chain with the dove charm.

Her heart was beating a mile a minute as she said, "Kelly gave this to Kaitlyn on her twelfth birthday. She never takes it off. She has to be here somewhere." She paused and yelled out, "Kaitlyn! Kaitlyn!"

Luke added his voice, and then they waited.

At first, all she could hear was the sound of the breeze through the trees. And then she heard a voice, a child's voice, filled with panic.

"Kaitlyn?" she yelled again. "Where are you?"

Luke was already moving down the path. She followed as quickly as she could.

"Kaitlyn," he shouted, stopping to peer down the hillside where it looked like some rocks had recently been moved.

"I'm here," Kaitlyn cried.

Liz looked over the edge, and her heart jumped into her throat. Kaitlyn was about fifteen feet down the steep hillside, her arms wrapped around the thick root of a tree that had fallen sideways against the mountain; it was the only thing stopping her from falling onto the jagged rocks a hundred feet below.

"Oh, God," she muttered, her heart racing.

"We're going to get you, Kaitlyn," Luke shouted. "Are you hurt?"

Kaitlyn shook her head, but it was clear she was terrified. "My arms are tired. I don't think I can hang on."

"You can do it," Luke said, firmness in his voice. "Just keep your eyes on us."

Luke turned to her, his mouth set in a grim line. "Here's the deal, Liz. I have two ropes in my pack. I can throw one down, but I'm not sure Kaitlyn will be able or willing to let go of the tree and grab the rope."

"She could fall while she was doing that."

"Exactly. I'd like to go down and get her, but I need someone up here to anchor the rope, and help pull Kaitlyn back up. I don't think you'll be able to handle her weight."

She suddenly knew where he was going, and it seemed impossible to grasp. "I can't go down there. I'll fall. I'll kill us both."

"You won't. I'll tie one rope around your waist. I can hold you, Lizzie. I won't let anything happen to you. You can take the other rope with you and tie it around Kaitlyn. I'll bring her back up and then I'll bring you up."

"Oh, Luke, I don't know." She felt nauseous at the thought of going down that hill.

"You don't have time to think about it. There's no one else here. It's you and me. We can do this. We're a good team."

"Are we?" she asked, her mind spinning.

"You know we are. If you don't know anything else, you know that."

She swallowed hard. "Okay. I'll do it."

Relief filled his eyes. "Good." He set his backpack on the ground and started pulling out what he needed for the rescue.

Lizzie's palms were sweating, her heart was racing, and as she looked down at her niece, she felt dizzy. *What if she slipped? What if Luke couldn't hold her weight? What if Kaitlyn fell before she got there?*

"Lizzie," Luke said sharply, pulling her gaze to

his. "Look in my eyes. Trust me."

He was literally asking her to trust him with her life and also with Kaitlyn's life. But she did trust him. She always had.

"I do. I'm ready. Let's get Kaitlyn."

Luke felt real fear for the first time in forever. It was one thing to risk his own life; it was another to risk Lizzie's. But he knew this was the only way they were going to be able to save Kaitlyn. He would make good on his promise. He would bring them both up safely.

He dug into the dirt behind a boulder to give himself a place to stand and a huge rock to block his weight against. He tied the two ropes around his waist, then tied both ends around Lizzie's waist. Once she got to Kaitlyn, she'd undo the top rope and put it around Kaitlyn. Then he gave her instructions on how to make her way down the slippery, steep hillside.

He could see the fear in her blue eyes, and she was literally shaking. He wished he didn't have to put her in this position, but there was no other option.

He leaned over and kissed her hard on the mouth. "You're going to be okay, babe."

She nodded, biting down on her bottom lip. "I've never been this scared."

"That doesn't matter. You're courageous, Lizzie. You are stronger than you know."

"Do you really believe I can do this?"

He met her gaze. "Without one single doubt."

She let out a breath. "Then I better get to it."

She walked over to the edge, dropped to her

knees and started to climb down facing the hillside. He let out the rope as she made her way down.

She moved slowly, carefully, and he found himself holding his breath with every step that she took. It seemed to take forever. And he silently prayed that she wouldn't stop, wouldn't look down, wouldn't suddenly freeze. He had confidence in her, but he wasn't sure how much confidence she had in herself.

"Doing great," he called out encouragingly.

Despite his words, his heart was pounding like a jackhammer, and all he could think about was how he wished he'd told Lizzie he loved her. *Why hadn't he said the words?* He'd never had a problem saying them before. She was the one who'd had difficulty putting that commitment into words. But he hadn't said them—not last night, not now…and he knew why. He was afraid she wouldn't be able to say the words back to him, that somehow he'd be left holding his heart in his hands again.

What a fraud he was, telling her to be brave, when he was too cowardly to speak the truth. He would tell her—later—when she was safe, when she could trust that his words weren't coming just from fear.

"Almost there," he yelled down, adjusting his stance.

"I'm coming, Kaitlyn," he heard her say to her niece.

"I'm scared," Kaitlyn told her.

"We all are," Lizzie replied. "But we're going to be fine. Luke will make sure of that." She stumbled at the end of her words, kicking up some small rocks and dirt.

Kaitlyn cried out as some of those rocks hit her.

"Hang on, Kaitlyn," he yelled.

Liz was close. Another foot, and she'd reach Kaitlyn.

Then things were going to get even more difficult.

Eleven

—➤➤◄◄◄—

"I'm here," Liz said, bracing her feet against the fallen tree as she put a hand on Kaitlyn's arm.

"I'm sorry," Kaitlyn said, tears streaming down her face. "I wanted to prove I could climb to the top of the mountain, but then I dropped my necklace and when I went to look for it, I slipped."

"We'll talk about it later." She had a lot of questions, but now wasn't the time.

"How are we going to get up there?" Kaitlyn asked with wide-eyed skepticism.

"I'm going to put this extra rope around your waist, and Luke is going to pull you up. Then I'll come after you."

She undid the knot on the top rope with shaky fingers. She knew Luke wouldn't let her fall, and she had her feet braced against the tree; she just had to trust him and trust herself. When she finally got it undone, she moved a little closer to Kaitlyn and somewhat awkwardly managed to tie the rope around her niece's waist. She made the knot that Luke had showed her and checked it twice to make sure it was strong.

"You're good to go," she said, forcing a smile on to her face. "All you have to do is scramble up the hill. Luke will pull you along."

"What if I trip or I fall?"

"He won't let you fall."

Kaitlyn stared back at her. "I couldn't do it before. I couldn't climb up the hill. I couldn't save Mommy. She told me to get out of the car, to look for help, but I couldn't do it. I was too scared."

The words tumbled out of Kaitlyn's mouth and Liz was shocked by a story she had never heard. The first people on the scene had said that Kaitlyn was sitting on the ground next to the car and that her parents had died on impact. But now Kaitlyn was telling her that Kelly had been alive.

"I'm the reason Mommy died," Kaitlyn said.

She shook her head. "No, honey, that's not true. Your mother's injuries were severe. She wouldn't have lasted more than a few minutes. She knew you loved her, and the last thing she would have wanted you to do was put yourself in danger to save her. She probably just wanted to get you out of the car in case there was a potential for a fire or for the car to slip farther down the hillside. You were the most precious person to her. She adored you, Kaitlyn."

Kaitlyn's gaze wavered. She wanted to believe; she just didn't know how.

"This isn't like before, Kaitlyn. You're not alone. Luke is on the other end of this rope. He will get you to safety. I promise you that. You have to trust me, honey." She realized she was saying the same thing to Kaitlyn that Luke had said to her. Maybe that's what all relationships came down to—trust and belief in the other person. "Let go of the tree, Kaitlyn—take my hand. I will not let you fall, and neither will Luke."

She put out her hand. Kaitlyn let go of the tree and then quickly grabbed her hand. "That's good. Now, the other hand. Put it on the ground in front of you." She braced her feet against the trunk as Kaitlyn freed herself. "She's ready, Luke," she yelled.

"So am I," he said. "Just climb up the hill, Kaitlyn. Don't look down."

Kaitlyn gave her one last look of indecision and she smiled reassuringly. "See you at the top."

"Promise you're coming back," Kaitlyn said. "I can't lose you, too."

"I promise," she said, her heart turning over in her chest. "You and I are sticking together."

Kaitlyn took in a deep breath and started to climb as Luke pulled on the rope to help her get up the hill.

Lizzie held her breath as her niece made her way up the slippery, rocky hillside. A few stumbles and heart-stopping pauses, and then she was safe.

"She's okay," Luke said, peering down at her. "Now it's your turn, Lizzie."

She was heavier than Kaitlyn and probably not as nimble, but she had to remember what she'd just told her niece. *Trust in Luke. Trust in herself.*

"I'll help," Kaitlyn said, moving next to Luke.

Kaitlyn put her arms around Luke's waist, and it was the most touching thing Lizzie had ever seen. She felt an overwhelming rush of love for both of them. They would not let her fall.

She made her way back up the hill, thankful for the rope around her waist pulling her up with assured confidence. When she reached the top, she scrambled away from the edge and took several ragged breaths before Kaitlyn hurled herself into her arms.

They hugged for several long minutes. And for the first time in forever, Kaitlyn was the loving, affectionate girl she'd once been.

"Hey, my turn," Luke said, wrapping his arms around both of them.

She wanted to stay in this warm circle of love forever, but they needed to get off this mountain before dark. She pulled away, and gazed up at Luke with so many words she wanted to say but no time to say them. So she settled for, "Thanks."

"You're welcome," he said with a smile, letting go of her, but not stepping too far away. "I'll make a rock climber out of you yet, Lizzie."

"I don't think so. That adrenaline rush will last me a good long time."

"It does feel a little good though, doesn't it?" he teased.

She had to admit that conquering her fears and climbing both down and back up did make her feel rather triumphant. "Maybe a little," she conceded. "Now let's go home."

"You've got it." Luke collected the ropes and put them back in his pack and then led the way down the path.

Lizzie took Kaitlyn's hand when they had enough room to walk side-by-side, and when they didn't, she followed close behind her niece, keeping Kaitlyn safely between Luke and herself.

When they got back to Wolmer Falls, they took a break by the pools. Luke pulled out water bottles and they each took long, welcome drinks.

"So, time to fill me in," Luke said. "I didn't hear

much of what you and Kaitlyn were talking about."
He turned to Kaitlyn. "Why did you come all the way
up here by yourself? Were you looking for the gold?"

Liz knew Luke was curious, but she wanted to
protect her niece from his questions, in case they
triggered more bad memories. "It's okay. She doesn't
need to talk about it now," she said quickly.

"I can tell him," Kaitlyn said. "I—I want to tell
him, and I want to tell you."

"Okay," she said, thinking she'd gotten past the
heart-pounding stuff, but maybe not.

Kaitlyn licked her lips as she faced both of them.
"I was thinking about the accident today because it's
my mom's birthday. I pulled out the photo albums and
when I saw how happy we used to be, it made me sad,
and it made me angry."

"That's understandable," she murmured.

Kaitlyn licked her lips. "The night of the accident,
my parents were arguing in the car. It was really late
at night and we were driving through the mountains.
My mom had wanted to leave earlier, but I was at a
party with some other kids, and I wanted to stay, and
my dad said it was okay." She drew in a breath. "On
our way home, it started to rain, and it was hard to see
out the windows. Mom was scared. I was feeling sick
because the road was so curvy. And then a car came
out of nowhere, and the lights blinded me and Dad,
too, I guess. My mom screamed and then we crashed
through something and we were flying. The car
flipped over a couple of times, and I was crying and
crying. I thought we were all going to die."

Lizzie's heart tore apart at Kaitlyn's words.
Kaitlyn wasn't just describing what had happened to
her but the last few moments of her sister's life. A part

of her wanted Kaitlyn to stop, but another part of her wanted her to keep going.

"When we finally stopped, we were at a slant. The front end of the car was smashed against the trees. Daddy's eyes were closed, and there was blood coming down his face. Mommy was trying to get her seat belt off, but she couldn't. She told me it would be okay. She said I should get out of the car. See what was around us. I told her I would get help, and she said she was proud of me, that I was being brave." A tear fell from Kaitlyn's eye, and she wiped it away with the back of her hand.

"But I wasn't brave," she continued. "I got outside, and it was really dark and rainy. There was a big hill in front of me. I went over there, and I started to climb up, but I slipped, and then I was too scared to try again." She took another breath. "I went back to the car, and I was going to get in, but it started to slide so I jumped out. I tried to talk to Mommy through the window, but she wouldn't talk back. So I sat down on the ground. Then the firemen came and they took me up the hill, and I never saw Mommy or Daddy again."

Lizzie stepped forward and put her arms around Kaitlyn's trembling shoulders. "Oh, honey, I am so sorry you had to go through that. Your mom wanted you to be safe; that's why she told you to get out of the car. She wouldn't have wanted you to climb that hill if it was dangerous. I know that."

"But if I'd gotten to the road, maybe I could have saved them," Kaitlyn said, pulling away, anguish in her eyes. "I could have waved down a car, but I was too scared so I did nothing. I should have died with them."

She immediately shook her head. "No, Kaitlyn.

You deserve to live, and your mother and your father would want you to live. You were their greatest joy. I know they're watching down on you right now. They want nothing for you but happiness and a long, long, happy life."

"You should hate me. You lost your sister."

"Never," she said fiercely. "I don't hate you at all. It's not your fault what happened."

"But if I hadn't wanted to stay at the party—"

"You can't think of all the things that could have happened differently," she told her. "Your dad made the choice to stay later. It was just an accident. It wasn't anyone's fault. I'll tell you that as many times as you need to hear it in order to believe it. Because it's the truth."

"I came up here today because I thought if I could go past Last Chance Rock and be really brave, my mom would somehow know that I wasn't a coward."

"Your mom knows. It was her necklace, the one she gave to you, that led us to you. I think she was watching over you."

A look of wonder came over Kaitlyn's face. "Do you think so?"

"I do." She gave Kaitlyn another hug, then glanced over at Luke.

He was watching them both with compassion and kindness in his warm brown eyes.

"Sorry we put you in the middle of all this," she said.

"I'm not," he replied. "I'm glad I was here to help."

"Me, too." She wished he could always be there to help.

"Can we go home now?" Kaitlyn asked.

She was thrilled that Kaitlyn had finally referred to the lodge as home, but as they made their way down the mountain, she couldn't help wondering how long the lodge really would be home. Luke was an amazing man. He'd saved their lives. But would he keep the lodge just to give them a place to call home?

They made it back to the resort just past seven as the sun set behind the mountains and darkness fell. They'd barely stepped foot on the property when the first of the worried staff members saw their arrival and came running to greet them: Nancy from housekeeping, Tina from the front desk, Jeff the handyman, and Tom all hugged Kaitlyn and told her how happy they were she was back.

Kaitlyn seemed surprised at all the attention. She'd really had no idea that even with her bad behavior, the staff at the lodge cared about her and wanted her to be safe and happy. Liz had never been more proud of her employees. She tried to make light of the adventure, not wanting to put Kaitlyn through any more emotional explanations, simply saying that her niece had finally decided to try a hike, but next time she would go with someone.

After a quick stop to wash their hands, she and Kaitlyn met back up with Luke in the dining room. He'd already ordered everything on the menu, he told them with a laugh, which was fine with Liz, since she'd worked up quite an appetite in the mountains.

Val, the new interim chef, with their sous chef Michelle's help, had landed on her feet quite nicely, and soon they were digging into juicy barbecued ribs and chicken, salad, roasted vegetables, fresh fruit, and twice-baked potatoes followed by a three-layer chocolate cake.

Liz couldn't remember being so hungry. Kaitlyn and Luke also made fast work of the meal. After they finished eating, Kaitlyn went to take a shower, and Luke suggested they take their coffee up to the roof. She was happy to go with him. She needed some space to decompress and escape all the well-meaning questions from the staff, most of whom weren't buying the *Kaitlyn-just-wanted-to-go-on-a-hike* story.

When they reached the rooftop patio, she took a breath of cool, fresh air and felt immediately better. It was a lovely night, with temperatures still in the sixties.

She sat down on the bench and let out a sigh of relief. "This is good."

"I thought it would be," Luke said, sitting down next to her.

"I can't quite believe everything that happened since we were up here last night." As she finished speaking, her memories flashed back to the hours in Luke's bed. It seemed like a long time ago now.

"It's been a busy day," he said with a small smile. "And here I thought there'd be nothing going on."

"You brought the excitement with you."

"Not this time."

"That's true. Kaitlyn was a simmering pot just waiting to blow. I knew in my gut that her mom's birthday was going to bring up some problems; I just didn't know what to expect. And then Shari going into labor four weeks early was quite a surprise. Speaking of which…" She pulled out her phone. "I got this text when we were finishing dinner. It's from Brad. *Shari just gave birth to our baby girl. Both doing great."*

"That's excellent news."

"It is." She let out a breath as she put her phone back into her pocket. "I didn't even have time to worry about her, but I'm so happy she's all right. I'm also glad Val is a capable chef. Another small miracle. We've had several of those today."

"Yes, we have."

She looked over at Luke and felt a tremendous wave of affection and gratitude toward him. He'd been so calm, so confident, so unwavering through those panicked minutes when she'd realized the trouble Kaitlyn was in. "I don't know what I would have done without you today. I owe you big time."

"I think I like the idea of you owing me something," he replied, his lips curving into a smile. "But in all honesty, you did the hard part, Lizzie. You climbed down the mountain. You put your life on the line for Kaitlyn. All you."

"You're giving me too much credit. You had to pull us back up."

"No big deal. You're both lightweights."

"Well, I still can't quite believe it even happened. It's surreal. When I think of all the things that could have gone wrong, it makes my stomach hurt."

"Don't think about what didn't happen, only what did." He set his coffee mug down on the bench and then took hers out of her hand and set it down as well.

"I wasn't done with that," she protested.

"You'll get it back. But first, I want to collect on your debt." He leaned forward and touched her mouth with his in a kiss that was meant to be tender but immediately triggered a firestorm of heat within her.

When he lifted his head, she cupped his face with

her hands and brought him back to her, stealing another kiss from his lips before she let him go. "You taste like chocolate and coffee, two of my favorite things."

"So do you," he said with a laugh. "But you're my favorite thing."

Warmth ran through her at his words. Luke could definitely be charming when he wanted to be. "You're high on my list, too."

"Good to know, especially since I'm wondering if you kissed me the second time just to taste the coffee on my lips, my little caffeine addict."

She laughed. "You do know me well, but that wasn't the reason. I just…"

"What? You just what?"

"Missed kissing you. Last night reminded me of how much I missed it."

His eyes darkened. "I know exactly what you mean." He paused. "Can I tell you a secret?"

"Of course," she said, as a nervous tingle ran down her spine.

He grabbed her hands, his fingers tightening around hers. "Today was the first time I've watched anyone I care about take a huge risk. I've never had to do that before. I've seen friends get into some dicey situations, but that was different. They were trained and prepared and knew what they were up against. But watching you go down that rope, I felt a worry beyond anything I've ever experienced. It is so much more difficult to watch someone face danger than to do it yourself. I don't think I ever knew that before."

Her heart swelled at the look in his eyes. "Last night when I was watching your movie, I wondered what it would have been like to be with you while you were taking all those tremendously dangerous risks. I don't know if I could have lived through it."

"Well, I now understand that worry better. This afternoon, when you disappeared over the edge, all I could think about was that I didn't want to lose you. I didn't want the world to lose you. I didn't want Kaitlyn to lose you. You're just too important."

Her heart skipped at his words, the depth of emotion in his voice. "That's nice—"

He cut her off with a shake of his head. "It's not *nice*. It's love." He paused, letting the word sink in. "I love you, Lizzie. I don't think I've ever stopped loving you. Even through the anger, it was still there. I just buried it so I didn't have to keep hurting."

Her breath stalled in her chest. "I—I—" She wanted to say she loved him back, but those words had always been difficult for her. She'd been so destroyed by the father who had abandoned her that telling another man she loved him and then watching him walk away had been beyond her. That old fear was part of the reason why she'd walked away from Luke first, because deep down she'd known it was only a matter of time before he would go, and she hadn't thought she could take it.

"You can't say it, can you?" he said with disappointment.

"You know I care about you."

"You can say you love coffee, but you can't say you love me?" He shook his head in bewildered annoyance. "That's fine. I didn't say it just so you would say it back. I know it's not a word you seem able to use with me."

"And you know why," she reminded him, because unlike any other man in her life, Luke was the one who knew her backstory, who knew her fears, her scars.

"I'm not your father."

"I know that." What she didn't know was why she was stalling. It was three simple words. But what would come next? What would happen after she put her heart on the line? She'd been so brave earlier, but now she was back to being a coward.

"Aunt Liz?" Kaitlyn's voice came from the stairwell, then she appeared on the roof. "What are you guys doing up here?"

"Just getting some air," she replied, pulling her hands away from Luke's. "Are you going to bed?"

"In a few minutes." Kaitlyn paused, giving them both an uncertain look. "I kind of wanted to talk to Luke, if that's okay."

"It's fine with me," Luke said.

Realizing that Kaitlyn wanted to speak to Luke alone, Liz got to her feet. "I need to check on some things downstairs. Say good-night when you come back down," she told Kaitlyn. "Luke—we'll talk later."

"Sure," he said in a casual way that erased the intensity of the last few minutes.

Was that because Kaitlyn was there or because she hadn't had the guts to say she loved him?

She mentally kicked herself all the way downstairs. But it wasn't over, she told herself. She would talk to Luke again. She would tell him how she felt. Even if he left, even if he broke her heart...

Twelve

Luke smiled as Kaitlyn sat down on the bench next to him. She'd changed into leggings and a sweatshirt, and with her hair down and damp from a shower, no hint of her usual heavy makeup, she looked very much like a young, sweet girl.

"How are you doing?" he asked.

"Okay." She looked around. "I've never been up here before."

"Really? Never? It's a perfect place for stargazing." He turned his gaze upward. "I always feel good when I can see the stars. It makes me feel like the world is bigger and that my problems are very small. And away from the city, the stars shine so much brighter, don't you think?"

"Yeah. There are a lot out tonight. Not like LA where I used to live."

"They're there—you just can't see them."

She nodded but didn't reply, and he didn't bother with another question. She had something on her mind, and she'd tell him when it felt right.

Finally, she said, "I miss my parents."

"I know." He paused. "I miss mine, too, and I'm a lot older than you. I don't need a mom and a dad anymore, but it still feels wrong that they're gone."

"Do you remember your mom?"

"Not as well as I wish I did. I was seven when she died. My memories are fleeting, but even when I can't really see her face, I can hear her voice, and I can remember the way I felt when she was with me. I was one of seven kids, but I always felt like she saw me. She saw each and every one of us." He took a breath, then added. "It was different with my father. To him, I think we were just a pack of boys. Sometimes when I'd get in trouble he couldn't even remember my name. He'd run through a couple of my brothers' names before he'd get to me. Although, he rarely started with James. James was my perfect older brother. I was nowhere close to perfect."

"What did you do that was bad?" she asked curiously.

"A lot of things I shouldn't have done. Luckily, I often had a brother looking out for me. That probably saved me a few times."

"I wish I had brothers or sisters. Then I wouldn't be so alone."

"You've got Lizzie," he reminded her.

"I know, but she—she should hate me. I've said some mean things to her. I hurt her feelings."

"But she doesn't hate you. She loves you like crazy. You need to let her in, Kaitlyn. She's not going to try to take your mom's place, but you can give her a place of her own, can't you? She'd die for you. She proved that today."

"I know. I couldn't believe it when she climbed

down the mountain to get me. I never thought she was brave at all. I mean—she's afraid of spiders."

He smiled and tipped his head, remembering all the spiders he'd killed for Lizzie. "You're right. She hates spiders. But we all have fears. It's how we deal with them that matters. And if you'd landed in the middle of a nest of spiders, she still would have gone down that mountain for you, because she loves you. You're her blood. She will do anything for you. I hope you know that now."

"I do." She licked her lips. "I wasn't very nice to you, either, when you caught me with Rex and Will."

"I'll give you a pass on that one, but I hope you don't make that mistake again."

"I won't. I know it was stupid to go with them. I don't even like them that much."

"I'm glad you know it was stupid. You're in a fragile state right now. You need to let the people around you protect you. Your aunt wants the best for you and so does everyone else around here. In case you didn't notice, you have a lot of supporters here."

"I don't know why," she said in bemusement.

He smiled. "Because you're young and you've suffered a terrible loss, and everyone can see that your anger covers your pain. But I also see a lot of strength in you, Kaitlyn. You've got guts. And you've got passion. You just need to let your brain into the mix."

"I was scared when I went past Last Chance Rock, but I thought if I could get to the top, I would feel better. I would make my mother proud again. But I didn't make it."

"I think you got to exactly where you needed to be," he said.

"What does that mean?"

"One of the Sherpas on my Mt. Everest climb told me that he sees more people fail than succeed, but they never go home a loser, because they got where they needed to go. They learned what they needed to learn. For some, that's a mile up. For me, I had to climb the whole damn mountain."

Kaitlyn grinned. "What did you learn from doing that?"

He thought for a moment. "That life is amazing and sometimes short but always worth the effort. I never just wanted to survive; I always wanted to live in a big way. I wanted to experience everything I could. That's why I do what I do and why I make movies so I can take people with me on the journey. I want a big life for you, too, Kaitlyn. Lizzie wants that as well."

"I don't know about a big life," Kaitlyn said doubtfully.

He laughed. "You're right. She probably wants a safer life than you might want, but that's just until you're grown up and ready to be on your own. Until then, she wants to love you and protect you and that might be smothering at times, but it will be worth it."

"I guess. I did kind of like hiking more than I thought I would, at least before I fell."

"You should go again, but not alone."

"Maybe with you?" she asked hopefully.

He hesitated. "Maybe. I don't know how long I'll be here."

"Are you going to sell the resort?" Kaitlyn asked, changing the subject. "I heard Shari talking about it."

"I don't know. I've never owned property before. I've never wanted roots. But I do like this land and this house and the mountains around us. What do you think I should do?"

"Keep it," she said immediately.

"So you do like it here?"

She shrugged. "It's not as bad as I thought."

He thought that was probably as much of a ringing endorsement as he was going to get.

"Aunt Liz wants to stay here," Kaitlyn added. "I think she wants you to stay here, too. She likes you."

"I like her, too."

"Then why don't you know what to do?"

"It's complicated. I spend a lot of my life traveling."

"You could still travel. And then when you come home, you could come here."

She made it sound so simple. On the other hand, was he making it too complicated? "I don't know how often that would be," he said slowly.

Kaitlyn suddenly cocked her head to the right. "Where's that music coming from?"

He heard the faint strains of a piano, and his pulse leapt.

He jumped to his feet and walked toward the stairwell. Kaitlyn followed him down to the living room. They paused in the doorway, as Lizzie played the piano she swore she'd never touch.

Seeing her fingers fly across the keys and the look of intense concentration on her face and her joy in her music, took him back in time to all those days he'd watched her practice. He'd known her talent was immense, that her big dreams could come true. Maybe that's why he'd been so insistent that she spend the summer with him. Subconsciously, he'd sensed her destiny lay somewhere else. He'd wanted to keep her as close as he could. He'd wanted her to live his life instead of her own. He just hadn't realized it until now. Thank God she'd had the sense to stand him up so many years ago. She'd been able to live her dream for at least ten years.

"Wow, she's really good," Kaitlyn murmured. "I had no idea."

"She's amazing," he agreed.

Within minutes, other guests and staff workers began to drift into the living room. Lizzie didn't seem aware of anything but the piano. She'd finally given herself permission to play it, and now there was no stopping her.

The impromptu concert ended about a half hour later. Applause broke out, and Lizzie looked up in surprise. She gave an awkward, self-conscious nod, then got to her feet, waving aside the compliments.

"Can you teach me to play?" Kaitlyn asked when she came over to them.

"Of course," Lizzie said, surprise in her eyes. "I'd love to teach you to play."

"I didn't know you were that good," Kaitlyn said. "Mom used to say you were, but I didn't know."

"Thanks, honey."

"I knew you were good," he put in, drawing her gaze to his. "You haven't lost a beat, Lizzie."

"It felt both strange and wonderful to play again."

"I thought you weren't going to touch the piano."

"After I left you both on the roof, I felt restless, and when I came downstairs, the piano called to me. I went to the one place where I knew there was peace. For me, that's always been the piano. It's where I feel safe, where I feel like I know who I am and what I'm supposed to do." She blushed. "That sounds silly."

"Not at all," he murmured.

Their eyes met and held for a long moment. Then Kaitlyn interrupted them once again.

"Can I talk to you, Aunt Liz?" she asked.

"Of course. Why don't we go upstairs?"

Kaitlyn nodded, then gave Luke a tentative smile. "Thanks again for saving me."

"You're more than welcome. Good-night."

Lizzie lingered behind. "We need to talk, too, Luke, but I don't know how long this will take."

"It's fine."

"Is it fine?" she asked doubtfully.

"You should go talk to Kaitlyn."

She frowned. "You're not leaving tomorrow, are you?"

He really didn't know. He probably should, because unless what she wanted to talk to him about was how much she loved him, he really didn't want to hear it. "I don't have any plans yet."

"Then I'll see you in the morning."

He nodded and watched her go, not at all sure he would see her tomorrow morning or any other morning.

He felt like he was right back where he'd once been—faced with uncertainty that Lizzie had ever or would ever love him enough to follow him or even ask him to stay. Was it that she just couldn't say the words, or because she didn't feel the love? But he knew she did; she was just afraid. Or maybe he was the one who was afraid. He could say he loved her, but he'd never offered her the life she really wanted. Could he do that now? Even if he did, would she say yes?

—➤➤◄◄—

Kaitlyn had already crawled under the covers when Liz walked into her bedroom. Judging by her niece's drooping eyelids, the stress and emotions of the day were catching up to her.

She sat down next to her on the bed and gave her a smile. "You look like you're about ready to fall asleep."

"I feel so tired all of a sudden."

"Me, too. We can talk tomorrow."

"I wanted to say something tonight. I wanted to tell you I'm sorry that I said Mom was mad at you for not coming home. She wasn't really. She was proud of how good you were at playing the piano; she just missed you."

"I missed her, too, and I do wish I'd gone to see you all more often."

"And I'm sorry I've been so mean to you. I thought…" She licked her lips. "I thought once you knew that I didn't climb up the hill after the accident, that I could have maybe saved my mom and dad's lives but didn't, that you'd hate me."

She immediately shook her head. "No, honey, I told you before that you couldn't have saved your parents even if you'd climbed two mountains. I really believe your mom told you to get out of the car because she was afraid it would slide farther down the ravine or burst into flames. She wanted you to be safe. That was her only thought at that moment. She wanted you to live. That's all that mattered to her. I know Kelly as well as I know myself. The proudest, happiest moment in her life was when she had you. I know that for a fact."

Kaitlyn's eyes watered, and she felt her own eyes tearing up, but she'd finally been given a chance to talk to Kaitlyn, and she had a few more things to say. "I want the same thing for you," she continued. "I feel this incredibly strong protective instinct toward you, and I know I'm just your aunt, but I want to make sure that every dream your mom ever had for you comes true. And I know those dreams were for you to live a happy, loving life. So that's what we're going to do, okay?"

"I just miss her so much. And my dad, too. It didn't feel right that I was alive and they weren't."

"It isn't right, but it's life, and we have to keep going. We're not going to forget them. We're going to remember all the little details and celebrate their lives every chance we can. I think that will be good for both of us, don't you?"

Kaitlyn nodded. "It was her birthday today."

"I know. And I think we gave her a good present."

"What's that?" Kaitlyn asked in surprise.

"We're talking—you and me. She'd want that more than anything."

"Yeah, she would," Kaitlyn admitted.

"You should sleep now. We'll keep talking tomorrow, right?"

"I have a feeling you won't shut up," Kaitlyn said with a hint of her old sarcasm, but there was love behind the words now.

She laughed. "That's probably true." She got up and walked to the door.

"Aunt Liz?"

"Yes?"

"Is Luke leaving?"

She drew in a quick breath. "I don't know when, but I think in the end he will leave."

"You should ask him to stay."

"I can't. He has to make that choice on his own."

"You're going to be sad."

She would be sad, but she wasn't going to show it. "I think we've both had enough sadness for a while. Whatever happens, I'm going to be happy for Luke, happy that he's doing what he wants to do."

"If you didn't have me, you could go with him," Kaitlyn suggested. "Or you could play the piano again."

"I can play the piano here."

"Not if Luke sells the place. The new owner might not let us stay."

"I don't want you to worry. We are going to be fine. You and I are survivors. We will bloom wherever we land." She smiled. "Your mom used to say that to me when our mom used to move us around a lot, when things were tough. And she was right. Life is meant to be lived. You take whatever is thrown at you, and you do your best and you make it good. We are going to have an amazing life together no matter what."

As she left the room, her own words rang through her head. She just hoped she could live up to the promise she'd just made Kaitlyn.

———⋙⋘———

Luke's phone buzzed as he got out of the shower early Saturday morning.

It was a text from Knox. *When are you coming back? Got tickets to the Dodgers tomorrow night.*

He sighed, not sure how to answer even that simple question.

While he was thinking, his phone buzzed again, a text this time from his friend and business partner Pete Ramsay. *Got lucky. Studio time opened up for Tuesday morning. You in?*

He stared at the text, feeling paralyzed in a way he'd never experienced. His life was calling. Why wasn't he answering?

Setting his phone down, he got dressed and threw the few clothes he'd unpacked into his duffel bag. He was still debating whether or not he wanted to put it in the car when a third text came in. This one was from Gabe. *I have a potential buyer for the resort. Interested?*

His chest tightened. He was interested, wasn't he?

Dammit. He'd never had so much trouble making a decision before. He grabbed his backpack and duffel and walked out to the car and threw them inside. Then he started down the path to the lodge. He'd get breakfast, talk to Lizzie, then decide what he wanted to do.

He was almost to the lodge when he ran into Brad, who was just coming down the steps.

"Hey Luke," Brad said with a happy smile.

"I thought you were at the hospital. Congratulations, by the way."

"Thanks. You cannot believe how beautiful my daughter is. And Shari was as tough as nails. I have never seen a woman in so much pain, but she just killed it and brought our child into the world. I don't know how she did it."

"I'm glad they're both good."

"It was rough for a while, with the baby coming so early. They want to keep her an extra day or so to get her weight up and make sure everything is working properly, but Doc says not to worry."

"Then you shouldn't worry."

"Easy to say," Brad said with a sigh. "But I suddenly feel overwhelmed. How good of a father will I be? It occurs to me I know next to nothing about babies. And we weren't prepared to bring a baby home. We don't even have the crib up. I have to find some people to cover my tours. John already has a full schedule. There's suddenly a lot to do really fast." He paused. "Sorry I'm rambling. My brain is like scrambled eggs this morning."

"Understandable."

"So did Liz really climb down the mountain on a rope to rescue Kaitlyn yesterday or has that story been embellished?"

"She did exactly that. She was amazing."

"I had no idea she had that in her. Thank God you were there to rescue them both."

"Liz did the hard part."

"So any chance I could talk you into taking over my hiking adventures for the next week?" he asked hopefully.

He hesitated. "Sorry. I have to go back to LA. We're going into editing the next film, and studio time just opened up."

Brad nodded. "It was worth a shot. Do you know what you're going to do yet with this place? Are you putting it up for sale?"

He saw more worry in Brad's eyes. He held a lot of people's happiness in his hands, and it wasn't a feeling he was familiar with. He was used to only having to be concerned with himself. "I don't know yet."

"Okay. Well, I hope I see you around. If not, it's

been great getting to know you."

"Likewise."

Brad headed to his car while Luke started up the steps to the lodge, but as he neared the front door, his pace slowed. Lizzie was going to ask him the same question Brad had just asked—or maybe she wouldn't. She thought she already knew what he would do. She was bracing herself for him to leave. He'd convinced himself that's why she hadn't been able to say she loved him. She didn't want to put her heart on the line and watch him stomp on it. He needed to convince her he wouldn't do that, but first he had to convince himself. He had to know what he wanted, and he had to be sure.

He looked around, seeing Tom giving a riding lesson to a young boy, a group of teens laughing as they headed to the pool, and a car pulling into the parking lot filled with kids that reminded him so much of his last trip here. This resort was more than just land and buildings. It was memories and love, not just for his parents who had first fallen for each other here, but maybe for him and Lizzie.

"Damn you, Dad," he muttered. "Why did you have to make things so difficult?"

He pulled out his phone, looked at Gabe's text, and then punched in a reply.

I've made a decision.

Thirteen

Five days later, Lizzie knew how Luke had felt when she didn't show up at the airport ten years earlier, when she didn't answer her phone, when she hadn't had the guts to say good-bye to his face.

She'd thought he would say good-bye before he left the resort. He'd told her he loved her, so how could he just leave? But that's exactly what he'd done. He'd taken off before breakfast on Saturday. It was now Thursday, and she hadn't heard a word from him.

Would she ever see him again? She really had no idea, and the pain in her heart had settled into a steady ache that occasionally ran through her in sharper waves when she thought about him. It felt worse than it had the first time they'd broken up.

Sighing, she looked at the computer screen in front of her and tried to put Luke out of her mind and concentrate on work. She would continue to do her job until someone fired her. Hopefully, even if Luke had decided to sell the resort, it would take at least a few months. School had started a few days ago, and

Kaitlyn seemed happy enough about her classes and the potential of friends. The last thing she wanted to have to do was pull her out of school now and move somewhere else.

Which was why she really needed to know what Luke was thinking. She couldn't understand what was taking him so long. If he'd decided to leave, then she should have at least heard from one of the Brannigan lawyers by now. She supposed she could call them directly. On the other hand, did she really want an answer? At this point, no news was better than bad news.

Pushing back her chair, she stood up and walked out of the office. She needed fresh air, and while business at the lodge had slowed down since Labor Day, it was Thursday, and there were some guests checking in for the weekend.

As she entered the living room, she was happy to see Brad and Shari walking in the front door. Brad held a baby car seat in one hand, and their beautiful daughter was fast asleep.

She'd been to the hospital twice to see Shari, but she'd thought the baby would stay in the hospital a few more days.

"You're back," she said with delight as Brad set the car seat down on the big coffee table in front of the couch. She threw her arms around Shari and gave her a warm hug. "It is so good to have you home."

"Thanks. It feels good to be home."

She sat down on the couch in front of the baby and felt a yearning deep within her soul as she stared at the infant. "She's beautiful and perfect."

Shari sat down next to her. "I think so, too. I still can't quite believe she's ours."

"And I am outnumbered by females," Brad added with a laugh. "So the second one will have to be a boy."

"Let's not talk about a second child right now," Shari protested.

"Fine, I'll give you a few months," he said with a teasing smile. "I'm going to take our beautiful daughter to our cabin."

"I'll be there in a minute," Shari said. After Brad and the baby left, she turned to Liz with a questioning gaze. "So how are things around here? Is Val holding her own?"

"She's doing a great job. She's not you," she added quickly. "But she's a solid cook and she's getting the job done."

"I'm glad. And Kaitlyn—is the good attitude still holding?"

"Shockingly—yes. She's gone back to the girl I remember, and it is such a relief. She's talking to me. She even showed me her homework last night. She's still on her phone a lot, but she has new local kids she's texting now. There's a girl who lives about a mile from here, and she seems like a good kid. Her father is a doctor at the urgent care center in town."

"That's great. To think it just took a hike…" Shari teased.

"And both of us almost dying," she reminded her. "But that dangerous moment finally broke down the wall between us, so I'm grateful for it. I did tell Tom that he's now prohibited from telling the story about the rock at our campfires, and I'm taking the lure of hidden gold off our flyers."

Shari smiled. "I'm sure the story will still get around."

"Maybe, but I'm going to make it a little more difficult to hear."

"And Luke? What's happening there?"

Her breath caught in her chest. "I haven't heard from him since he left."

"We really need to know his plans," Shari said, concern in her eyes. "If we have to move, we need time."

"I know. I don't know what to tell you. I can try to track him down, but he could be anywhere in the world by now. And part of me thinks that it might be better just to wait, see what happens. Maybe he just hasn't decided, and he's letting things ride."

"I know it's complicated for you, Liz, but I think you might need to call him. Every one of the staff members who came to visit me at the hospital was concerned about their jobs. I'm afraid people will start looking for other positions just to protect themselves."

"I'm aware. I have the same concern. I'll give it until next week, then I'll look for him. I really hoped Luke might see this place as a good investment, or that maybe he might like owning a place in this beautiful valley. He's such an outdoorsman. But that was a fool's dream."

"Or the dream of a woman in love," Shari said gently, as she stood up. "You do love him, don't you, Lizzie? I saw the sparks between you right from the start."

She got to her feet. "It doesn't matter how I feel. Luke's life has always been somewhere else. And to be fair, mine has, too. We just can't get the timing right."

"Maybe that's about to change," Shari said.

"What do you mean?"

Shari tipped her head to the door behind her.

Liz turned around, shocked to see Luke walk into the room. Her stomach immediately clenched, and her head spun at the sight of his handsome face and rugged body. She hadn't thought she'd see him again. She'd really believed their next contact would be an email or a certified letter or maybe a text.

"Hi," Luke said, his gaze on her face as he walked forward.

"Hi," she murmured back.

"So, I'm going to go," Shari said.

"How's the baby?" Luke asked, dragging his gaze from Liz to Shari.

"She's beautiful. Brad just took her home. Come by later if you want to meet her."

"I will. Congratulations again."

"Thanks for the flowers you sent. They were beautiful."

After Shari left, Liz didn't know what to say, so she settled for something completely irrelevant. "You sent Shari flowers?"

He nodded. "It seemed like the right thing to do."

"That was nice."

"I can be nice."

He could be nice. He could be a lot of other things, too, but she didn't want to think about his good traits, only his negative ones. She had to prepare herself for bad news, so she needed to get her armor up quick. "It would have been *nice* if you'd said good-bye before you left."

"I thought about it. I was actually on my way into the lodge last Saturday when I decided I wasn't ready to say good-bye yet."

"So you just left?"

"I needed to think."

"About what?"

"You."

Her heart fluttered with impossible hope. "What about me?"

"Last week when Kaitlyn ran away, and you and I went past Last Chance Rock, I couldn't help thinking that that rock symbolized our relationship. It was our opportunity to forget the past and move forward. How many people get a second chance in life, Lizzie?"

"Do you want a second chance?" she whispered, trying not to get too carried away by his words.

"I do."

"But how could we possibly work? It's not like that much has changed. And what has changed doesn't tip the scales in our favor. You didn't want to stay before because the world was calling, and I didn't want to leave because my career was calling. But now I have Kaitlyn. It's not just me anymore. It's me and a thirteen-year-old who has already proven how much trouble she can be."

He smiled. "I think Kaitlyn has turned a corner. She's texted me a few times since I left."

"She has? She didn't tell me that."

"We didn't talk about you. She told me about school. It sounds like she's settling in."

"It sounds like you and she have become friends."

"I hope so." He stepped forward, his brown eyes dark, deep, intense, as he settled his hands on her hips. "I don't want to leave you again. I don't want to keep running around the world looking for something— someone—I've already found. That empty hole in my heart—only you can fill it."

She licked her lips. "Luke—"

"Wait. I'm not done yet. You can come up with a thousand reasons why you and I don't work, but the truth is we do work. We're incredibly good together. We balance each other out. We can talk about things that matter. We can laugh and play and be serious, too. I trust you, and I think you trust me."

"But—" she began.

"No buts," he interrupted, putting a finger against her lips. "If you can't tell me you love me now, then I'll wait—as long as I have to. Or maybe I'll just love you enough for both of us."

She was so overwhelmed by his words, her eyes started to water.

"I want to be where you are," he continued. "If that's here, then consider this my new address."

"Seriously? You want to live here?"

He nodded, a smile playing around his lips. "I do. I was thinking that we could turn the last un-remodeled cabin into a studio, and I could do my film editing in there. I could limit my filming to a couple of months out of the year. Maybe the summer months or winter break. Perhaps you and Kaitlyn could come with me on some of those trips—when school is out."

"You've thought about this a lot," she said, feeling amazed.

"Ever since I left here, I haven't been able to think about anything else."

"I really didn't believe you were coming back, Luke."

"And how did you feel about that?" he challenged.

"Incredibly sad." As his gaze burned into hers, she knew it was past time to tell him how she really felt. "I don't just want you or need you, Luke. I love you. I don't know why it's taken me so long to tell you that, because it's been true forever."

He drew in a sharp breath, and she could see that her words meant a lot to him. "You weren't ready to say the words before. I'm happy you are now."

"Me, too, because I don't want to lose you again, either. You are too important to me."

"Then we're finally on the same page."

"And the same continent," she said with a laugh.

He grinned back at her. "That, too." His humor faded as his expression turned serious. "I want you to know that I'm ready to put you first—you and Kaitlyn. Because my dreams now are really only about you, about being your husband and maybe a father figure for Kaitlyn."

She drew in a quick breath. "Really?"

"That's not a proposal. I'm doing that up right one day, but I just want you to know exactly what I'm thinking."

"And I want you to know that when you want to ask me, the answer is going to be yes. If it were just me and Kaitlyn wasn't around, I wouldn't ask you to stay here; I'd follow you to the ends of the earth. Because I know now that my life is never going to be completely right without you."

"I don't need you to follow me. I need you to be next to me. I want us to be together, whether it's me making a film or you playing in a concert hall or both of us watching Kaitlyn do something amazing."

"I want that, too," she said, her heart overflowing with emotion. She wrapped her arms around his neck and kissed him with all the love she was feeling. Then she said, "I can't believe this, Luke. I can't believe we're back together after all these years."

He smiled down at her. "And it pains me to say this, but my father was right. We were meant for each other."

"I guess he knew you better than you thought."

"I guess he did. I had a lot of growing up to do."

"So did I. I'm sad we missed years together, but I think we both needed to find our own way. Who knew it would be here—in a beautiful resort in the woods?"

"Certainly not me," he admitted. "But I am so ready for this adventure. I think it's going to be the best one yet." He paused. "So where's Kaitlyn?"

"At school. She won't be home til three. She's going to be very happy."

"Good." He glanced down at his watch. "Looks like we have about an hour before we can tell her the good news. I wonder what we should do with the time," he mused, a wicked smile on his face.

"It's the middle of the day," she protested. "I'm supposed to be working."

"I'll make it okay with your boss," he teased, as he stole another kiss. "Let me show you how happy we're going to be, Lizzie."

She let out a sigh as he ran his mouth down the side of her neck. How on earth could she resist a line like that?

"Show me, Luke. Show me now and show me forever."

"I will." He grabbed her hand as they ran up the stairs, like the two kids in love they'd once been and would be forever more.

THE END

Get the complete series:

Luke – Barbara Freethy (#1)
Gabe – Ruth Cardello (#2)
Hunter – Melody Anne (#3)
Knox – Christie Ridgway (#4)
Max – Lynn Raye Harris (#5)
James – Roxanne St. Claire (#6)
Finn – JoAnn Ross (#7)

—➤➤◄◄—

Also by Barbara Freethy

—➤➤◄◄—

About The Author

Barbara Freethy is a #1 New York Times Bestselling Author of 52 novels ranging from contemporary romance to romantic suspense and women's fiction. Traditionally published for many years, Barbara opened her own publishing company in 2011 and has since sold over 6.5 million books! Twenty-two of her titles have appeared on the New York Times and USA Today Bestseller Lists. She is a six-time finalist and two-time winner in the Romance Writers of America acclaimed RITA contest.

Known for her emotional and compelling stories of love, family, mystery and romance, Barbara enjoys writing about ordinary people caught up in extraordinary adventures. Romance Reviews Today calls her a "master storyteller". Library Journal says, "Barbara Freethy has a gift for writing unique and compelling characters."

For a complete listing of books, as well as excerpts and contests, and to connect with Barbara:

Visit Barbara's Website:
www.barbarafreethy.com

Join Barbara on Facebook:
www.facebook.com/barbarafreethybooks

Follow Barbara on Twitter:
www.twitter.com/barbarafreethy

Made in the USA
Middletown, DE
25 October 2016